# PRETENDING
## WITH THE
# GREEK
*Billionaire*

# PRETENDING
## WITH THE
## GREEK
## *Billionaire*

## KIRA ARCHER

Entangled Publishing, LLC
10940 S Parker Rd
Suite 327
Parker, CO 80134
rights@entangledpublishing.com

Indulgence is an imprint of Entangled Publishing, LLC.

Edited by Alethea Spiridon
Cover design by Bree Archer
Cover photography by dima_sidelnikov/Getty Images

Manufactured in the United States of America

First Edition August 2016

*For all those who provide good homes to amazing kids—may you find a few moments of peace and quiet to actually read this.*

# Chapter One

Luca Vasilakis stirred, sensing someone's presence near his ear. He really should open his eyes and see who it was, but the pounding already starting in his head made him rethink that decision. The faint aroma of garlic wafted over him and he grimaced, his stomach churning. It had to be Joseph, his personal assistant. The man put garlic in everything.

Before Luca could shoo Joseph away, he heard a quick intake of breath and then the word "Sir!" was shouted so loudly in his ear he was certain his head would explode.

Luca reared up from the chaise, his eyes squinting against the sun that seared his corneas. He brandished the champagne bottle in his hand like a weapon, hoping he'd get lucky and make contact with some part of Joseph's anatomy. Unfortunately, Joseph, pristinely put together as always in an impeccably tailored suit, his graying hair gelled into submission, stood out of range, waiting for Luca to pull himself together enough to remember where he was.

"What the hell are you doing, Joe?"

"We need to discuss the meeting with your father, sir."

Luca waved him off and took a swig of the champagne, grimacing when he swallowed it. "Cancel it."

"I did that moments before waking you, sir. You didn't look up to it. It has been rescheduled. But I was only able to buy you a few hours, I'm afraid."

He gave Joseph a wry smile. "I knew there was a reason I keep you around. Get someone to clean this up, will you?"

"Already done, sir."

Luca surveyed the utter destruction around him. Servants picked their way through the mess with garbage bags, rousing his guests and setting things back to rights. He let out a long, slow breath. Looked like last night had gotten a little out of hand. The raven-haired beauty who'd curled herself around him on the chaise stretched, the movement shifting her bikini in what should have been a tantalizing fashion. Luca barely noticed. He couldn't remember her name or anything else much about her. The only thing he was certain of was that they hadn't had sex.

He didn't do public displays of affection. Any displays of affection, really, and certainly not where some hidden paparazzi lens might capture it. He ran a hand through the unruly mane on his head, frowning when his fingers snagged. Apparently, someone had braided several clumps of his shoulder-length hair. He glanced down at one and swore under his breath at the bright blue ribbon threaded through the black strands.

"You have got to be kidding," he muttered. He made a new resolution—no more getting so drunk that someone could braid his hair with pretty ribbons without him noticing.

"Sir," Joseph said, picking his way through empty bottles and passed-out partygoers. "This can't continue. Your father is quite determined. You will lose everything if you keep on this way."

Luca waved him off, knowing he spoke the truth but not wanting to hear it at the moment.

"Sir," Joseph persisted. "The meeting with your father was rescheduled for later this afternoon. He also asked me to remind you…"

"I'm aware of my father's ultimatum, Joe. I shape up, grow up, find a nice girl, and settle down, or I'm out of a job, family, money…did I leave anything out?"

Joseph smiled. "No sir, that about sums it up."

"Well, then, let's save the rest of the dire threats for my father then. Wouldn't want to leave him with nothing to say."

"Yes, sir."

Luca rubbed his hand over his face. He'd better get cleaned up and over to his father's office. Keeping the old man waiting had never improved his temper. And while he'd made these threats before, something was different this time. His father seemed…fed up. Sad, even. This time, he might actually follow through.

Not that Luca had a damn clue what to do about it. He'd tried to curb his partying. Well, he could try harder in that department, but he certainly wasn't going to find himself a wife and settle down just to make his father happy. The last thing in the world he wanted was to be tied down to some nagging harpy determined to make his life hell. Time enough for that when he was past his prime and too old to have any more fun. For now, he'd say what he needed to appease his father and get on with his life.

Easier said than done.

Within moments of walking into his father's office he knew he was screwed. Augustine Vasilakis wasted no time on pleasantries. Not even a hello. He leaned back against his desk, his hands tucked with deceptive casualness in his pockets, and gave Luca the barest nod when he entered the office.

"Sit down."

"Father, I already know—"

"I'm aware of what you know. Now, let me tell you what *I* know. I know that despite all the advantages you've been given in your life, you've done absolutely nothing with them. I know if I don't do anything, you'll continue to waste that life on frivolous nonsense. And I know if I were irresponsible enough to hand this company over to you, you'd squander it away as well. So now let me tell you something you *don't* know."

Luca sat in silence. He'd never seen his father like this before. Oh, there had been the lectures on his poor life choices. More than he could count. But never had his father had such a cold, determined anger about him. Anxiety took a leisurely stroll through Luca's veins and set up camp somewhere in the vicinity of his sinking stomach.

"A meeting with the board has been scheduled for one month from now to announce the completion of our new locations in New York and Madrid. During that meeting, I am expected to formally give you control of our New York offices. I have no intention of doing so as things stand."

"What?" Luca nearly jumped from his chair, his stomach bottoming out. "You can't do that!"

His father's frown deepened. "I can, and I will." He sighed, his shoulders slumping a bit. "Luca, I did not come to this decision lightly. You are my son, but I will not allow you to destroy the company I spent my life building. I started from nothing and now I run one of the most successful international real estate firms in the world. The opening of our new offices could triple our holdings. New York is especially critical and with the right management should do very well, hopefully beyond our expectations, but not with you in charge. I can't jeopardize the future of this company."

"I wouldn't do that. I can run New York. Well."

"And why should I believe that? You've done nothing

since your mother died but party and drink and whore around the Mediterranean with an ever-increasing string of gold-digging party girls. Getting your face plastered all over the damned tabloids, and for what? I don't even know what it is you're supposed to be famous for. Dating some actress? Partying with musicians? Throwing your money around to impress people who don't care about you? If you want the fame, you should at least do something for it! Make something of yourself. Be successful at something other than managing to make a career out of being stalked by paparazzi."

"I don't encourage them. They just follow me."

"They'd stop if you'd stop giving them dirt to smear. I know it's too much to hope that you'll find some nice girl somewhere who will tame your wild ways, but it would be good if you'd try to find someone who won't make your mother roll over in her grave."

Luca took a deep breath, anger burning through him with such intensity he couldn't speak. Sitting there being reprimanded like a misbehaving child rankled worse than he'd thought possible, but beneath the anger, a thread of shame smoldered. He didn't like what his father was saying, but he wasn't wrong. And there was nothing worse than being called out on your shit when you knew you deserved it.

"I know I haven't always made choices you agree with…" His father snorted but Luca ignored it. "But I'm your son. I've been preparing for this my whole life. I know I haven't been around much lately, but I do keep up with things. I read all the reports, follow everything that's going on. I know this business inside and out."

His father sighed and walked back around his desk to slump into his chair. "Like I said, you've got one month to prove to me that it wouldn't be a mistake to hand you my life's work. I won't stand by any longer and watch you drink yourself to death. I'll fire you if I have to, if it means not financing your destructive lifestyle. You can live on your trust fund and whatever you've got left from your mother, for as long as that might last. You're almost thirty years old. You either pull your life together, or the job will go to someone else, and so will the company when I'm gone. Now get out."

Luca didn't argue. He didn't even open his mouth for fear of what he'd say. He simply stood and marched from the office, his father's words ringing in his ears.

Joseph drove him home in silence, Luca's mind too much in turmoil for conversation. When they arrived, Joseph opened his door. "You have a dinner tonight with Miss Lexington at eight o'clock and drinks and…entertainment following at Club Phoenix, then—"

Luca stalked into the house, waving him off. "Cancel everything. I'm staying in tonight."

"Sir?" Joseph said, his brow furrowed.

Luca almost laughed at his confusion. It was probably the first time he'd ever been told cancel plans. Luca, however, was in no mood for the frivolous company of his friends at the moment. And the beautiful Tiffany would have no trouble finding someone else to escort her to dinner. In fact, he wouldn't be surprised if she'd been meeting someone else later that night anyway.

"You heard me, Joe. Cancel everything."

"Yes, sir."

Luca tossed his sunglasses onto a table as he headed toward the back. With his so-called friends gone and the house peaceful and quiet, he could actually relax and think for a change, not something he generally liked to do, but he needed to come up with some way to get his father off his back that didn't entail changing his entire life. Maybe a few minutes soaking up the sun and staring at the amazing ocean view he paid through the nose for would spark a few ideas.

His shirt and shoes followed his glasses and his pants were

halfway unbuttoned when a shriek of laughter stopped him.

"Joe! I thought you got rid of everyone this morning."

"I did, sir," Joseph said, his forehead crinkling as the party-like sounds floated in from the backyard.

"Then what the hell…"

The nearer he got to the door, the more the shrieks and laughter filtered to him. Luca stepped off his back deck and down to the lower deck where the infinity pool looked out over the turquoise ocean and pristine white sand of his private beach. He stood, completely dumbfounded by the scene before him.

Half a dozen children splashed about in his pool while a woman in a white T-shirt and knee-length khaki shorts, wearing insanely ugly Velcro-strapped sandals, tried to haul them one at a time out of the water. She seemed to be succeeding more at soaking herself with water than she was getting the little heathens out of his pool.

"What is going on here?" he shouted.

The woman's head whipped toward him, the movement loosening the bun that held her dark red hair atop her head. She tucked the escaping tendrils behind her ear.

"Out of the pool, girls, now," she said, her voice brooking no argument.

The girls immediately obeyed, filing one by one from the water to stand behind their caretaker. Six pairs of young, terrified eyes looked up at him, a few pairs of lips quivering in the process. One little girl with a thick braid of black hair peeked out from behind the woman to stare at him. His eyes narrowed and she darted quickly back under cover.

The woman patted the girl on the head and whispered something to her as she pried the little one off her leg and handed her to one of the older girls. Then she straightened like she was off to face a firing squad and marched, chin in the air, toward him.

A grudging respect mixed with the anger coursing through him. There weren't many women who could stare him down when he was angry. He crossed his arms and waited.

"I'm very sorry," she said, her voice with its American accent somehow firm and soft all at the same time. "I realize we are probably trespassing…"

"Probably? How did you even get in here? Do you make a habit of sneaking onto other people's property and—you! Get out of there!" He pointed at one child who was hip deep in his bushes, several flowers clutched in her hands. "Joseph, do something."

"What did you have in mind, sir?" Joseph asked, eyebrows raised.

"I don't know. Just…" He waved his hands like he could make the whole scene disappear. It didn't work.

"Elena, get down from there! Put those down right now," the woman said, hands on her hips like some anal-retentive schoolteacher.

"Look, I don't know who you are…" Luca said.

"Constance McMurty," she said, sticking her hand out like she was at some job interview.

He shook it automatically before he realized what he was doing. Her fingers were warm and soft against his own, but she shook his hand with a firm grip, no nonsense. Exactly two pumps and then she let go.

She looked at him expectantly with deep sapphire blue eyes that gazed directly into his. Those eyes narrowed and he realized she'd asked him something, but he hadn't a clue what.

"This is Mr. Vasilakis," Joseph said, reliable as always. "This is his property."

"*Luca* Vasilakis?" Constance said before taking a slow, deep breath.

Good, she'd heard of him. Well, maybe not so good. None of the stories that circulated about him were entirely true.

Most were grossly exaggerated if not downright fabrications, and none of them were flattering. Luca frowned, wondering where the sudden urge to put his best foot forward was coming from. What did he care what this woman thought of him?

"I'm so sorry," she said. "One of the kids wandered in and I…"

"Thought you'd bring the others in for a dip in the pool?"

"No, of course not."

He raised an eyebrow, taking in the six dripping wet children gathered behind her.

"Well, they did go in the pool, but they weren't supposed to. Elena wandered in," she said, pointing to the smallest child, the little girl with a dark braid running down her back who had been digging up his flowers. "I had to come in after her, and I couldn't leave the other children outside the gates by themselves. So… well, I…we came in and then they saw the pool and they were hot and one of them went in and then the others…well…"

"How did you even get in? Climb the gate?"

Her mouth dropped open with a gasp of outrage. "Of course not! I would never. The gate was open."

Luca shot a glance to Joseph, his anger spiking. It was hard enough keeping the paparazzi and curious tourists at bay. The last thing he needed was for his gates to be opened wide and welcoming them in.

Joseph frowned. "I will check on it, sir."

Luca glanced back at the girls, his frown deepening. He didn't like being around children. It wasn't that he disliked them especially. They were just so small, and messy, and noisy. *And destructive*, he thought, looking at the one who'd torn up his flowerbeds.

"Well," he said, clearing his throat, unnerved a bit by all the feminine eyes staring at him. The bright, blue pair belonging to the crazy mother hen of the group in particular. "If you all have finished with your swimming for the afternoon, perhaps you could…"

Before he could finish, the buzzing noise he'd heard faintly in the background grew to a roar.

"What the fu—"

"Mr. Vasilakis, watch your language, please!"

Luca stared down at Constance in astonishment. Had she really just chastised him for swearing, in his own home, where she was trespassing? His lips cracked into a grin, despite himself. It had been a long time since anyone had surprised him.

The roar grew louder as a helicopter rose from behind the rock hills his house nestled against, close enough the blades sent gusts of wind tearing through the backyard. The girls all shrieked, some scattering toward the house, the others tackling Miss McMurty's legs. Knocked off balance, she threw out her arms and he reached to catch her. She landed neatly in his embrace, clutching at his biceps for support.

The helicopter flew out of sight, but Luca knew they'd circle back around in a minute. Damned paparazzi. They weren't supposed to get that close. He couldn't get rid of them, though he supposed he was partly to blame, since he always managed to give them something good to report. You'd think they had enough pictures of him joyriding through town or at a restaurant with some woman. Partying with people he had no business being with, whose only goal in life was to get in the papers no matter what stupid thing they had to do to accomplish it. He let himself get pulled along a few too many times. Some of his finest moments, right there. Just at that moment, however, he was having a hard time thinking about anything but the woman in his grasp.

She fit against him perfectly, like she'd been made especially for him. She gazed up at him, her breath coming in sharp little gasps. Her shirt was still damp and the water had made the fabric tantalizingly see-through, just enough that he could make out the outlines of a spectacular pair of firm, round breasts. The faint scent of cherry blossom rose up to meet him. God, she smelled good.

Her lips parted and he leaned closer. She didn't back away, her eyes riveted to his mouth. Her breathing kicked up a notch and she lifted her face ever so slightly. Well then…

Luca's head dipped down and she jerked back just before he made contact.

"What are you doing?" she asked.

"You seemed like you were expecting a little something extra," he said, not letting her go. "I thought I'd indulge you. Wouldn't want to be a bad host, after all."

He leaned toward her again but she slapped a hand against his chest. "The children will see!"

Luca grinned. His body blocked her from the kids' view. She should be a lot more worried about the damn helicopter that was probably on its way back.

"Excuse me," she said, but before she could say anything more, the helicopter circled back around, its roaring motor shattering whatever strange moment they'd had. The wind from the blades kicked up sand, dirt, and debris and he pressed Constance's face against his neck to protect her face from the flying particles. He held her close and pressed his lips to her ear so she could hear him.

"Let's get inside!"

Constance nodded and pushed away from him but he kept his arm around her waist, guiding her toward the house. The helicopter disappeared over the roof, but wouldn't be out of sight long.

"Wait!" she said. "We're missing one."

Luca turned around just in time to see the little one who'd torn up his flowers topple into the deep end of the pool. He reached the pool in three strides, his heart in his throat, and jumped in, holding onto the side with one arm while snagging the little girl with the other. She came up sputtering. He hauled her into his chest and heaved them both out of the pool. Constance was there, arms out, but the child wouldn't let go of his neck. The helicopter loomed again, the photographer leaning out the open door with his camera. Luca swore under his breath and turned back to the house. He'd pry the child off his neck inside, away from the vultures.

Joseph helped herd all the kids inside, closing the doors and drawing the drapes the moment they were all safely in.

The little one in Luca's arms coughed and he awkwardly patted her on the back. "Water is for swimming in and drinking, not breathing. Let's try to keep it out of our lungs next time, hmm? Might be best to stick to the shallow end for now, eh *paidi mou*?" he said, the term of endearment slipping from his lips.

*My child*…just like his mother used to call him when he'd done something silly or naughty. He hadn't thought of it in years. He shifted uncomfortably and pulled the girl away from his neck.

He handed her over to Constance, who stood by with a towel that Joe must have grabbed for her.

She nodded up at him with wide eyes while Constance dried her off.

"Thank you," she said, hugging the child close. If you hadn't been there…"

He frowned and waved off her thanks, his discomfort growing. Having both of them staring up at him was more scrutiny than he wanted to deal with just then. "Don't worry about it."

"We need to go," Constance said. "We can't be here with… that," she said waving toward the sound of the retreating helicopter. "I'm sorry about trespassing and…out there. I mean that we almost…that I…" Her fingers fluttered to her lips and Luca's stretched into a slow smile, his momentary agitation fading with the memory of his near brush with her lips. She flushed a red nearly as deep as her hair. "You nearly…that was…"

"Pleasant?"

"Unexpected."

"Pleasurable."

Constance stiffened. "Unwelcome."

"Unlikely," Luca said with smug confidence.

Constance's mouth dropped open and it was all Luca could do not to haul her back into his arms and show her how much she would have enjoyed it. He chuckled and she glared at him.

Well, if nothing else, this little escapade had given him the diversion he'd desperately needed after seeing his father, even if it probably made things worse. That alone would have bought the intriguing Constance some mercy from him. The tantalizing near taste of her lips went a great deal farther.

"Joseph, please escort Miss McMurty and her charges home."

"Oh please," she said, "that's not necessary at all."

"I insist," Luca said.

She opened her mouth, probably to argue again, but the faint sound of the helicopter still overhead must have changed her mind.

"All right then." She turned to Joseph. "Thank you."

"My pleasure, miss," he said with a little bow. "Follow me."

She gathered everyone up and started to follow Joe out to the garage where Luca had several vehicles of varying sizes waiting for his use.

"Until next time, Miss McMurty."

She turned back toward him, her eyes flashing blue fire.

"Goodbye, Mr. Vasilakis."

Luca found himself smiling as she disappeared around the corner.

*What the hell had just happened?*

# Chapter Two

Constance held the phone to her ear with a trembling hand. Although with the way her director, the Mother Superior of the tiny convent on Mykonos and the head of the Emergency Family Aid group on the island, was screeching she probably could have left the phone across the room and heard her fine. With her other hand, she scrolled through the pictures that had been filling the internet for the last several hours.

Her. Surrounded by the kids. In Luca's arms. It didn't matter that nothing had happened. That he had only been shielding her from the dirt the helicopter had kicked up. It looked as if they were eating each other's faces.

*Pleasurable*? That deep, smug voice of Luca's replayed over and over through her head.

Yes, damn him. It had been pleasurable. Being pressed against that rock-hard body had almost been enough to make her forget where she was, forget the girls were there, forget there was a helicopter full of bloodthirsty paparazzi with long-range lenses. Forget everything but the warm strength of those arms around her. Those insanely full, soft lips mere millimeters from caressing hers. His tightly corded muscles bunching beneath her fingers. The soft and rough mixture of tanned olive skin with its oh-so-trendy stubble rubbing across her face.

Pleasurable enough to nearly make her forget herself. Lose control. And now it didn't matter that she hadn't given in. It looked bad enough. The fact she was even on his property would be enough to put her position in jeopardy. Risk the only thing in life she really loved. Her kids.

She'd wanted to be part of the Emergency Family Aid program since she'd first come to Greece and heard about it. She already had a degree in social work, and even though it was through an American university, it had given her a leg up. Finishing the training the program required so she could be a House Mother for a group of children hadn't taken long. She'd been with her six girls for over a year. Their placement with her was meant to be permanent, and if she lost them because of one stupid mistake, she'd never forgive herself.

She sucked back a renegade sob and tried to focus on the fury coming from the phone. She'd already had one scathing phone call from her father. That's just what every girl wants, to explain to Daddy why it looks like she's rounding second base with the resident Casanova with six kids looking on. She had a nice, traumatic brunch to look forward to the next day as well. Apparently she'd screwed up severely enough he felt the need to cancel all his appointments and jet right over to check on things in person. Just lovely.

And now she got to go round two with her director, a nun, about the so-called steamy pictures all over the internet.

"Yes, Reverend Mother, I understand. But it's not what it looks like…I mean it sort of is but…we were there…but the rest…I didn't…"

She stopped, knowing she was only making it worse. She might be able to explain why she was in the man's backyard, but the shots of her locked in his embrace were a little more difficult. It didn't matter that she hadn't been kissing him. Just the appearance of wrongdoing was enough. And she *had* been trespassing on private property with her children. Unavoidable as it had been, it was still illegal.

The Reverend Mother wrapped up her chew-out and clicked off. Constance was to report to her office the next morning for a formal meeting with the Reverend Mother, Ms. Castellanos, the head of their particular group of homes, and Mrs. Ballas, the woman who worked with Constance and helped her care for the girls. They were to discuss her actions and possible removal as a House Mother.

Constance sank into a chair. She knew the second she'd laid eyes on the glowering Greek god that he was trouble. She wished she could rewind time and listen to her gut. It had never failed her and going against it bit her in the butt every time, but what else could she do? She couldn't have left Elena wandering about on his property anymore than she could have left the other children on their own while she went to fetch her. Of course, had that been the whole of it, this wouldn't be an issue right now. It was her conduct with the most notorious playboy bachelor in the Mediterranean, in front of the girls, that was the issue, and rightly so. She should have shoved away from him the moment he'd gotten near her. Maybe she deserved to lose them.

The only good thing from all this was that Luca wasn't pressing charges for trespassing. He was infamous for a lot of things, not the least of which was being lethal when it came to keeping his private property private. He did what he could to keep his property off limits, although that was apparently shockingly little. Enough torrid details about his personal life made it into the papers that he either had poor friends or a leak somewhere in his staff. It almost made her pity him.

He couldn't keep the paparazzi from spying on him with

their long-range lenses from boats in the ocean waves that butted against his property, or the helicopters that invaded his air space, but those who dared to step foot on the property were dealt with swiftly and harshly.

There hadn't been a word about that, however. He'd even had his personal assistant drive them all home, a courtesy she was sure he didn't offer most trespassers. Maybe that almost-kiss had bought her a little leniency. Would it be too much to hope that it might buy her a little more?

Before she could talk herself out of it, Constance threw her shoes back on and ran next door, knocking until Mrs. Ballas stumbled to the door.

"What is it? Is it one of the girls?" she asked.

"No, but I need to run out for a minute. A quick errand. Could you come keep an ear out for them?"

Thankfully, Mrs. Ballas was too tired to question her much. She was at Constance's and snoring on the couch before Constance could grab her keys and lock the door behind her. She jumped onto her beat-up old scooter and headed out. If there was one person who could set the record straight, it was Luca. Maybe she could get him to speak to her directors, tell them it wasn't as bad as it looked, that it had been his fault.

Constance pulled up to the gate outside Luca's property and pushed the little button on the call box.

"May I help you?"

"Mr. Stavros, is that you?"

"Indeed it is. To whom am I speaking?"

"This is Constance McMurty, from earlier..."

"Ah yes. Miss McMurty. What can we do for you this evening?"

"I was hoping to speak to Mr. Vasilakis. It won't take long."

"One moment please."

Constance gripped the handlebars while a thousand

octopi flopped around in her stomach.

"Mr. Vasilakis would be happy to speak with you," Joseph said. There was a loud clicking sound and the scrolled metal gates opened to welcome her in.

"Oh God, here we go," she muttered, easing her scooter through the gates and up to the main house.

She didn't have any time to steel herself to see him again. When she got off her moped, Luca stood in the open doorway, leaning against the jamb with his arms folded across his bare chest. Her gaze traveled over his body, a little shiver running through her as she took in the soft flannel pants that barely clung to his corded hips, and nothing else but a solid expanse of kissable skin. His thick, black hair hung in damp tendrils to his shoulders, like he'd just stepped out of the shower. The scent of his soap, something musky and masculine, grew stronger the closer she got to him and she had to resist the urge to sniff the air like some rabid bloodhound.

When she got nearer, he padded toward her on bare feet, not stopping until he was only a few inches from her. Constance craned her neck to look up at him.

"Stanzia, you've come back for another visit?"

"Constance," she murmured. "My name is Constance, though I'd prefer if you'd call me Miss McMurty."

"But I wouldn't prefer it. Much too reserved for the woman who fell into my arms this afternoon. Stanzia is softer, sweeter on the lips." He glanced at her mouth and it was all she could do to keep from tucking her lips in, away from his heated gaze. "It shall be my pet name for you."

Constance frowned and backed away from him. "You don't know me well enough to give me a pet name. It's Miss McMurty. We need to speak about this afternoon."

Luca stepped aside and held his arm out. "By all means, enter."

She hadn't really noticed her surroundings earlier when

they'd run inside to escape the helicopter. The simplicity of the space surprised her. Inside was well lit, tastefully decorated, completely harmless looking. So why did it feel like she'd been welcomed into some depraved den of sin?

Joseph welcomed her with a huge smile. "*Kalispera*, Miss McMurty. May I get you something to drink?"

"Good evening, Mr. Stavros. No, thank you. I'm fine."

"Call me Joseph, please."

"Call me Constance," she said, smiling at him. Him, she liked. His boss on the other hand…

"You allow him to call you by your given name?" Luca asked, brow furrowed in consternation. Or was it amusement? Why did he always seem to be either irritated or laughing at her?

"He has been nothing but courteous and respectful. He's earned the right to use my given name."

The eyebrow quirked up again and this time she definitely detected amusement. The man was insufferable.

Luca's arm brushed against hers as he walked by her and she shivered again. How did the merest touch from that man do that to her? He sprawled on the large white leather sofa and gestured to the matching overstuffed armchair facing him.

"Have a seat."

She perched on the edge of the chair ready to run at the first sign of any funny business.

His lips twitched as he settled back against the cushions and she narrowed her eyes. He had her number and he knew it, and despite her best intentions, there didn't seem to be a damned thing she could do about it. Best to get on with her business and get the hell out of there before she let her severely neglected hormones totally ruin her life.

"So what can I do for you?" Luca asked, his dark brown eyes and slowly smiling lips insinuating there was much he'd like to do to her…er, for her.

"Have you been online at all tonight?"

"Not tonight, no."

Constance took a deep breath and nodded. "Well, there are photos of us…from earlier…"

"Oh?" Luca's smile was full blown now. "And what exactly are the pictures of?"

Constance huffed, already done with the game. "You know very well what they are of. I want to know what we can do about it."

"Do? Why should we do anything? They're pictures. Ignore them."

"I can't ignore them! Because of those pictures I might lose my girls."

Luca's amusement faded. "What girls? The ones who were here? They are yours? All of them?"

Constance glared at him. "My directors think I brought my charges here and exposed them to…"

Luca's eyebrow rose a notch.

"Well, brought them here so I could…so we could…"

Luca's brow rose higher and Constance glared at him. "I'm sure you can figure out what they think."

"I'm sure I can, too. Maybe I want to hear you say it."

"Mr. Vasilakis," she said, her temper overriding her determination to keep herself under control.

"Call me Luca."

"I'd rather not."

"Why?"

She frowned again. "Because I don't know you well enough."

That damned eyebrow rose again. "I think we know each other well enough for first names. Besides, I wish it."

He sat back as if that decided the matter, and she opened her mouth to argue the issue with him, and then reminded herself there were more pressing matters than what she'd call him. Especially since she didn't intend to see him again after tonight.

She closed her eyes for a brief second and composed herself, drawing in a deep breath and straightening her back. But she opened them to find Luca's gaze boring into her with an intensity that sent a shudder rippling through her. Maybe if she avoided looking directly into those impossibly dark eyes she'd be able to get through this. She looked instead at the slight dimple in his chin.

"Mr. Vasilakis, I came to ask if you would speak with my directors on my behalf. Explain to them that nothing happened."

"That might be rather hard to explain considering the images they've seen," he said with a laugh.

She glared at him. "You said you hadn't seen the pictures."

"No, I said I hadn't been online tonight. I didn't say I hadn't seen the pictures."

He reached over to a stack of printouts on the table next to the couch and handed her a tabloid from the top of the pile.

"I don't normally read these, either, but Joe thought I might want to see these so he took the liberty of printing out a few articles from a few of the more thorough sites."

The top page showed an overblown, up-close image of her in Luca's arms, bodies pressed together from head to toe, looking like she was extremely happy to be there. She should have taken the face-full of dirt. It might have hurt, but it would've saved her a lot of trouble.

"Oh God," she groaned. "I'll be sacked for sure."

"Maybe not," Luca said, a tone in his voice that Constance couldn't identify.

"What do you mean?" she asked, afraid to hope he'd actually agree to help her.

"I have a proposal for you."

"What kind of proposal?"

Luca turned to Joe who stepped forward. Constance frowned.

"Mr. Vasilakis is in a bit of trouble of his own," Joseph said. Luca grimaced but he didn't interrupt. "His father wishes him to"—his gaze flicked to his employer and he appeared to be choosing his words carefully—"live a more sedate lifestyle."

Luca snorted.

"Well, I can understand that, but what does it have to do with me?"

Luca gestured to the tabloid Constance had dropped on the coffee table. "Some enterprising peon in my father's employ saw the pictures of us and did a little digging on you. Seems you are a fine, upstanding young woman with no warrants, arrests, or blemishes on your record of any kind. Moreover, you have dedicated your life to help those less fortunate and are currently working as a House Mother in one of the children's village homes where you spend your days looking after orphans and foster children. My father is over the moon."

Constance's frown deepened. "I can't possibly see why."

"You are the type of woman with whom he'd love to see his son settle down," Joseph said. "One who might 'tame Luca's wild ways' as I believe he put it."

The thought of even attempting to tame Luca sent a thrill through Constance she couldn't quite contain. But she'd be damned if she let him see it.

"I'm flattered," she said drily, "but again, I don't see what your father has to do with me."

Luca leaned forward, resting his elbows on his knees. "I'll help you out of your mess if you help me out of mine."

Constance drew in a careful breath. "What does helping you out of your mess entail?"

"Our company is set to open its new offices in New York.

If I want to run them, as I have been anticipating, I need to prove I can settle down and start 'behaving like a responsible adult' as my father puts it. Otherwise, the job will go to someone else and so will most of my shares in the company. I'd like to avoid that if possible."

Constance nodded. Sounded reasonable enough, although she still wasn't sure how she could help.

"You, I take it, would like to keep your position and remain with your charges."

She nodded. "Yes."

"So my proposal is that for the next month you pose as my fiancée."

Constance's mouth dropped open, but for the life of her she couldn't make herself speak. If he had told her his plan was to have her dress in feathers and parade around town clucking like a chicken she couldn't have been more surprised.

"I…I…" She took a deep breath. "How does that help you?"

"It gets my father off my back. If I'm engaged to a respectable person such as yourself, he'll assume my old ways are behind me. We play up the lovebird act for a month or so until I've been made president of the New York offices and am in full control of my shares, and then we both go back to our own lives."

"How is that supposed to help me?"

"I'll speak to your director, tell her that you were bringing the girls you care about so much to meet me, at my request. If we are engaged, it would be natural for them to meet me as I would become part of their lives as well. It still might not be ideal for them, but it's better than the alternative: that you brought the girls with you so you could trespass on private property and once there, accost the poor, unsuspecting owner—a much-sought-after celebrity—with your young charges watching."

"But that's not what happened!"

"It's only a slight twist of the truth and the pictures support the story."

"That's blackmail!"

"I choose to see it as helping each other out."

"You can choose to see it any way you wish. It's blackmail and you know it."

Luca shrugged. "What choice do you have?"

Constance fumed, fury flooding every cell in her body until she nearly vibrated with it. She took a deep breath, struggling for calm. "What *exactly* would this charade involve?"

Luca leaned back against the couch with a smug look that Constance itched to smack off his face. He waved at Joseph, who came forward and handed her a stack of papers.

"I will have a contract drawn up, complete with a nondisclosure agreement similar to this." He handed her the papers. "At the end of the month, well, six weeks because your association will need to extend at least a week or so past the date Mr. Vasilakis is approved for the position, your relationship will dissolve. At that time, you'll be free to go your separate ways with the stipulation that neither of you reveal any details about the relationship and its validity or anything that took place during the time of your association. You'll need to spend a great deal of time with Mr. Vasilakis, of course."

"But the girls…this isn't a babysitting job. I'm their legal guardian. Their mother for all intents and purposes. They live with me. I can't disappear for six weeks."

Joseph jumped in. "The girls are welcome to accompany you, of course."

"Joe," Luca snapped. "We've already discussed that."

Constance frowned, not understanding.

Luca filled in the gaps for her. "Joe feels my hanging out with orphans will help drive home the message that I've changed. A little extra PR."

She glared at him. "You are *not* going to use my children as some sort of prop for this ridiculous farce."

"Of course not. I've already told Joe no pictures."

"I wasn't suggesting they be used as…props, for lack of a better word," Joseph said.

"Good," Constance ground out, her threshold for politeness rapidly disappearing. "Because I absolutely won't allow that."

"No, no, of course, not," Joseph said. Then he turned back to Luca. "But as they must stay with Miss Constance and we need her with us, it stands to reason…"

Luca sighed. "Yes, so you've said before."

"No." Constance folded her arms. She wasn't backing down on that point.

Joseph tried again. "We will do our utmost to keep the photographers away from them, certainly. Our interest is in *you*, Miss Constance. However, if it were to be known that they were spending time with Mr. Vasilakis…"

"No," she said again, standing firm.

"If they will be here with you anyway, I don't see the harm in leaking that fact," Luca said. "I agree there will be no pictures of them. But a few stories about them hanging out with me won't traumatize anyone. They will never be directly involved. They seemed to be having a grand time earlier today. Do you really think being taken on trips and getting to swim in my pool is going to upset them?"

"That's not the point," she said.

He released an exasperated sigh. "It's exactly the point. They aren't going to be damaged or mistreated. *No orphans will be harmed in the making of this film*," he said, making those ridiculous finger quotes.

She could almost hear the eye roll in his voice. "I thought you didn't want them here."

"I don't. But I do need you here. And at least the illusion that I'm spending time with the kids wouldn't hurt either. If letting them hang out by the pool for a couple days gets me a little respectability, I'm willing to make the sacrifice. I doubt very much they'll mind."

She hated to admit he was right. Given the choice, the girls would jump at the chance to hang out in his pool and go on more excursions. Yet it still worried her. Luca's lifestyle wasn't one she wanted them exposed to, even if they did manage to keep the photographers at bay. Something she doubted was possible.

"I suppose appealing to your decent side and asking you to help me out with no strings attached wouldn't help?"

"Sorry. I don't have a decent side that I'm aware of."

She glared at him. "I need some air."

She stood and marched through the kitchen and onto the back patio. The scene of the crime where the whole fiasco started. She groaned and plopped onto a chaise with her face in her hands.

What in the hell was she supposed to do? If she walked out of there, she'd be facing her director the next day and would very possibly lose her girls. She would do anything for them. Take a bullet, jump in front of a bus, whatever it took to keep them safe and happy. In that context, spending a few weeks being treated to all the luxuries life had to offer in order to keep their family intact really didn't sound all that bad. As long as it was understood her girls would not be used as paparazzi fodder. Underneath it all a tiny part of her, the part she didn't like to acknowledge existed, was even excited by the thought of spending so much time with the enigmatic and completely annoying Luca.

Regardless of how she felt about it, he was right. She didn't have a choice, not if she wanted to keep her girls. *Son of a bitch.*

She took a deep breath and marched back into the house, resuming her seat. Luca and Joseph looked at her, eyes wide and waiting.

"I don't want my girls in any questionable situations," she said.

"No, no," Joseph said. "We'll have several activities planned, outings the two of you can take them on, picnics, days at the beach, that sort of thing. I promise they will enjoy themselves."

She had no doubt that they would. That wasn't the problem. The problem was them having too much fun. Getting too attached to a lifestyle, and maybe a man, that they couldn't keep. She wouldn't allow anything that might hurt them down the road. They'd been through enough in their lives to dangle such a shiny carrot only to yank it away.

"I wouldn't want the girls to know what's going on. For them, if I agree, it can be just a fun vacation that has a beginning and an end, with a man who is just a friend. No fake couple stuff in front of them."

"I'm not sure that will be possible if we are to get the publicity we need." Joseph shifted his feet and glanced at Luca.

"Minimal then," she said with a sigh. "Nothing that would make the kids think it is real. They're going to have to go back to their old lives and I'm not going to let them be hurt by any of this. It'll be hard enough to go back to the real world when the vacation is over. I'm not going to let them get attached to someone they think might be sticking around. I don't think it's too much to ask to keep it PG around them."

After a quick glance at Luca, Joseph nodded. "Not at all." He gave her a kind smile and she blew a breath out. "Now, you'll need to move onto the estate for the duration of your engagement in order to facilitate intimate photo opportunities and make the relationship appear more realistic."

"You want me to move in?" Constance asked, looking between the two of them. She wasn't sure if it was horror or excitement that made her legs shake like palm fronds in the wind.

"You may have your own room, of course," Joseph started but Luca interrupted him.

"No. You'll share my room."

"What?" Constance asked, completely taken off guard.

He leaned forward, elbows on his knees and a dangerous twinkle in his eyes. "And my bed."

Even Joseph's eyes widened at that one. Constance stared at Luca, barely able to draw breath. He returned her gaze, stone-cold serious for once. His entire body was tense, his muscles clenching and unclenching like he was trying to prevent himself from jumping up.

Her mind shouted angry obscenities at the arrogant jerk even as her body nearly trembled at the thought of being in such close proximity with him.

She shook her head, her words coming out more as a whisper than the forceful declaration she'd meant them to be. "You can't blackmail me into having sex with you."

Luca's lips twitched into a half smile. "I've never been that hard up, love. I didn't say that we'd be having sex, though I'm certainly open to that any time you wish."

Constance glared and gritted her teeth. Luca just grinned and continued on. "I said we'd share a bed. Despite Joseph's vigorous screening process and more nondisclosure agreements than I can count, somehow the intimate details of my life still manage to get leaked to the tabloids on a distressingly frequent basis. If we're going to make this look real, you can't live with me in a room down the hall. You'll have to share my room, and my bed, like my real fiancée would. Well, *almost* like a real fiancée. I assure you, your virtue is safe from me. As long as you want it to be."

She shook her head, thankful she had a legitimate reason they couldn't argue with to get out of his twisted little plan. "I can't do that. I told you, I can't abandon my children. Moving in here would certainly fall under that criteria."

"Why do you keep calling them your children? What, you adopted them all?" Luca asked, his forehead creased.

"No, but the arrangement is similar. It's possible the girls who still have families might return to their homes one day, but it's highly unlikely. Releasing children to the program is a last resort step for most families. Only undertaken if there are no other options, no other means of support, because in order to create safe, stable environments for these kids, it's necessary to give them permanent homes. Permanent caregivers. Keep them from being bounced back and forth."

"So you signed up to take care of six kids, permanently, all on your own."

She frowned slightly at him. "I can't believe you've never heard of this program before. It's not like it's some secret organization."

"I've heard of it. Not the specifics, but I know the gist."

Constance shook her head. "And that's the problem right there. If more people like you knew, or cared about more than the gist about programs like this, we wouldn't need programs like this."

His eyebrows rose. "So people like me should…what? Go adopt everyone?"

"No, but it wouldn't hurt for you to be a little more involved."

"Maybe. Depends on your definition of involved."

It was her turn to raise an eyebrow. He held his hands up in mock surrender. "Hey, not all of us are cut out to parent half the island."

Her lips twitched despite herself. "I didn't know I'd end up with six children, but we don't like to split up sibling groups. I've got two sets of siblings. And Elena. And I don't do it entirely on my own. In some locations, House Mothers live near each other, some even in special villages built for the purpose, in order to give each other support and additional stability for the children. There isn't anything like that on Mykonos yet, though I hope there will be one day. For the moment, I live next door to a widow, Mrs. Ballas, who helps me."

"So why can't this Mrs. Ballas watch them for a few weeks while you stay here?" he asked, stretching out his long legs. His bare feet were inches from her own legs and she shifted a bit so he wasn't quite so close. He gave her a smug smile that she ignored.

"She helps out, kind of like a housekeeper. But I told you I am their mother. I wouldn't leave them to someone else for several weeks for no good reason any more than I'd do that with my own biological children. This program isn't like a typical foster care system, certainly not like the one in America. I'm not technically an adoptive parent, but the program does make me legally, physically, morally, and spiritually responsible for my girls for the rest of their lives. Well, technically until they're legal adults. But I'm not going to raise them as my own and then walk away once they are eighteen. I'm not just going to walk away from them for weeks on end either."

The last thing the girls needed was to see the woman they depended on ditch them for a month to go shack up with some guy. They'd seen too many people in their lives walk away, and not come back. She'd never do that to them.

She'd been young when she'd been left at an orphanage herself, but she remembered standing there, knowing she'd been left, knowing she was alone in the world. When her adoptive parents had come along, it had been better for a while. And then her mother died. She'd been abandoned again. She still had her father, but after her mother's death, he'd been different. Too wrapped up in his own grief to realize the pain his daughter was in. Realize that to her it was like being left at that orphanage all over again.

She'd never voluntarily leave her girls for any length of time, for any reason, but she didn't need to explain her reasoning. It was none of his business.

Luca shook his head, looking at her like she was crazy. "And your family had nothing to say about you doing this? Throwing your life away for a bunch of kids you have no real ties to?"

Constance glared at him. "I did not throw my life away, and yes, my family was a little shocked when I decided to become a part of the program."

That was an understatement. It had been like she'd announced she was having a child out of wedlock…times six.

"They got over it. Look, I know *some* people," she said, pinning Luca with a glare again, "might find this…unusual. I knew what a huge step I was taking, basically adopting six kids. But the need is so great. So many children need homes, someone to love them, care for them. And they've been nothing but a blessing in my life. Caring for my sweet girls was the best decision I'd ever made."

Luca shook his head again. "Seems like it would put a damper on your social life."

She sighed. Yes, it made the prospect of dating nearly impossible. There weren't many men who were willing to date a woman with six children in tow, but that didn't matter all that much to her. "I don't expect someone like you to understand. I've never regretted my decision. I'm not just going to ditch my girls to come play house with you."

"Fine. They can stay here too then. I've got a whole guest wing that is never used. There is more than enough space. Besides, wouldn't opening my home to orphans buy me some bonus points?"

The calm and collected Joseph actually did a double take look at his boss. She guessed neither of them saw that one coming, but then he pursed his lips and nodded. "Strictly from a PR standpoint, it couldn't hurt."

"Of course it would hurt!" Constance said, her mind reeling. "How am I supposed to keep the girls from thinking this whole thing is real if we are all staying in your house and I'm sleeping in your bed."

Luca shrugged. "They'll be on the opposite side of the house, and you seem the type to be the last one in bed and the first one awake."

She grimaced at him. "You say that like it's a bad thing."

"It is. In any case, I'm sure it'll be easy enough to keep our sleeping arrangements from disturbing the little darlings. Tell them you're sharing a room with your housekeeper woman. They won't know the difference."

The man was crazy. Insufferably crazy. End of story.

He blew a breath out. "I've never had to work so hard to get a woman into my bed," he muttered.

Constance rolled her eyes. "I bet." He winked at her and she stifled an exasperated groan. "I am not sleeping in your bed."

"Have it your way. There is a sofa in there. Should be comfortable enough for you."

"I'm the guest. Maybe you should take the sofa," she mumbled.

The half grin was back. "Hey, I offered you the best bed in the house. The offer still stands."

She almost answered his smile with one of her own. It was disturbingly difficult to keep brain on the right track when he was trying to be charming. "If it comes with you in it, I'll take the sofa."

He shrugged. "Suit yourself."

"This is insane." She rubbed her temples.

"You act as though I'm asking you to stay in some condemned shack. Would it really be such a sacrifice to stay here for a few weeks?" he asked, gesturing at the luxury that surrounded them.

It wasn't staying in the house that bothered her. It was staying with *him*. But as she had no intention of admitting that she ignored the question. "I don't know if I'd even be allowed to bring them," she said.

Luca waved that comment off. "I'll make sure it's all arranged with your directors. A sizeable enough donation should make any objections go away."

Constance shook her head. She couldn't possibly, although, the house was gorgeous and huge. And she would love for her girls to get to experience living in a place like this. It might make it more difficult to return to their modest home. Perhaps, as long as she made it seem like a holiday…

She couldn't believe she was entertaining the thought, even if there was a certain logic to the plan. That didn't mean she had to like it. Only she was afraid that that was the problem. Somewhere deep inside, she *did* like it. Some long neglected part of her was nearly crying for joy at the thought of belonging to this man. It was a part she was going to need to tear out by the roots if she was going to get out of this in one piece.

"So," Luca said, his face once again relaxing into his usual smug expression. "What's it going to be, Stanzia? I'm going to be calling your directors one way or the other in the morning. What will I be telling them?"

Constance stood, praying her legs would support her long enough to get her to her moped.

"Fine. You've got yourself a fiancée."

# Chapter Three

Constance checked her watch for the fifth time and scanned the street again, even though there was no way a car could have come in without her seeing. Just great. Luca was supposed to have walked into the office with her, a solid, united front to help give their ridiculous story a little credence. Instead, she'd have to slink in there on her own, since he couldn't be bothered with showing up. If she lost her children, their deal was so off. She took a deep breath and walked into the building to face the music.

Within five minutes, she was sitting before her director's desk, praying the cold sweat she was sure hovered near the surface of her skin would stay put long enough for them to spin their load of crap and get out of there. The grim countenances of the Reverend Mother, Ms. Castellanos, and even Mrs. Ballas didn't give her much hope for that, especially as Luca still hadn't deigned to join her.

What if he'd changed his mind? Gotten a call from his dad or someone that the charade wasn't necessary so he'd decided to call the whole thing off and hadn't bothered to tell her? He wouldn't do that, would he? Just bail on her like that?

The fact she even questioned whether Luca would hesitate to ditch her showed how far past her usual defenses he'd already gotten. Of course he would bail on her. Bailing is what Luca Vasilakis did best. Just ask his father…or the dozens of perfectly formed models he'd dated and then discarded when his interest ran out.

Constance tried to swallow past her suddenly dry mouth as the Reverend Mother stared her down until she wanted to curl up in a hole and die. And still Luca didn't show.

"Miss McMurty, I'm afraid we can't wait any longer. Apparently, Mr. Vasilakis has thought better of joining you if indeed he ever intended to be here in the first place."

Constance's mouth dropped open but the Reverend Mother gave her no leeway to defend herself.

"We've called you in today to discuss your shocking behavior yesterday. Your conduct until now has always been above reproach. What possessed you to behave in such a… reprehensible fashion, I have no idea, and in front of the children, no less."

Constance tried to think of something to say but before she could the door opened and in breezed Luca. Pure relief blew through her. He hadn't ditched her after all. The identical expressions of shock that graced the faces of the three women at the desk would have been comical if the girls she loved weren't on the line.

"Sorry I'm late, darling," he said, marching over to her.

Before she could respond, he bent over, captured her face in his hands, and kissed her, hard, fast, and so thoroughly that all four women in the room, Constance included, were gasping and clutching their figurative pearls by the time he was finished. Constance grabbed at his shirt, meaning to shove him away yet somehow only pulling him closer. The smug and completely male sound of his low, deep laugh hit her right in the belly and spread like fire.

She blinked up at him, completely blindsided. What the *hell* had that been? And how was it possible to be so pissed off and completely turned on at the same time? She wanted to slap him for thinking he had the right to touch her like that...and push him up against the wall and make him do it again. It took her a second to shake off the haze of hormones his lips had unleashed and pull herself together. He grinned at her and pressed a much more chaste kiss to her forehead.

Anger won out over desire. How dare he march in there and ambush her like that? In front of two of the most conservative women on the island and her friend, who looked like she wasn't sure if she should applaud or shout for help.

Luca looked like he'd just rolled out of bed. His rumpled hair looked almost artfully tousled though it was probably the result of just having left his pillow. The morning scruff on his chin only enhanced the sexy bedroom vibe he had going on. It was unfair for someone to look that appealing without any effort.

"My apologies if I kept anyone waiting," he said to the still-stunned trio behind the desk. "Had a little bit of business to take care of, and I've got quite the full day scheduled so I'm afraid this will have to be brief."

He took Constance's hand and pulled her from the chair.

"Mr. Vasilakis," Reverend Mother said, only a slight stammer to her voice.

Constance was impressed. It took a will of steel to keep one's composure in front of *the* Luca Vasilakis.

Reverend Mother continued. "We'd like to offer our sincere apologies for any inconvenience the actions of Miss McMurty may have caused..."

Luca interrupted her. "There's no reason for apology. My fiancée had merely brought the children to my estate, at my request, so that I could meet the charges she's so fond of."

He pulled her into a one-armed hug that squeezed the breath from her lungs. "She goes on and on about them." He gave her a loud kiss on the cheek and she tried to glare at him with her eyes without letting her anger show on the rest of her face. She must have partially succeeded because an amused grin spread across Luca's lips.

"Your fiancée?" Ms. Castellanos sputtered.

"Yes. Didn't Stanzia tell you? Ah, that's my little duckling. So modest." He chucked her under the chin with his finger and Constance had to grit her teeth to keep from biting him. If he didn't tone it down, he was going to blow it.

He must have realized she was nearing the end of her very frayed rope because he loosened his grip on her waist and turned back to the women at the desk, his demeanor sobering. A little.

"Well, ladies. As I said, we have quite the busy day planned. I only wanted to stop by and make sure there was no confusion about what happened yesterday. Everything is on the up-and-up and all that."

"Yes, I suppose…"

"Also, I hope it won't be too much of a bother, but we thought we'd best give it a bit of a trial run with the children. They'll be staying at my home for the next several weeks. I know I need to go through all the proper paperwork once we are married and the children will be with us full time, but we thought a bit of a holiday on my estate could help ease them into it. Mrs. Ballas, of course, is invited as well."

Mrs. Ballas turned bright pink and stammered out a response, but Constance knew she was excited. The Reverend Mother didn't look quite as pleased.

"Well, I don't know if that's…"

"You know," Luca said, interrupting again. "I've always found the work you do here admirable. I've been meaning to make a nice donation for some time now. I guess no time like the present, eh? I'll have my assistant deliver a check this afternoon if that suits you."

"Oh. Yes, that would be wonderful, Mr. Vasilakis. How generous."

He waved her off. "Speak nothing of it. It's a deserving cause. I'm happy to do it. Now about the children. If it's too much trouble, I suppose we could…"

"Oh, well…" Reverend Mother patted at her hair and straightened her necklace, more flustered than Constance had ever seen her. It wasn't every day a woman got steamrolled by the force of nature that was Luca Vasilakis, she supposed.

"No, not at all," she finally said. "I'm sure the children will enjoy themselves. As long as Mrs. Ballas accompanies them as well, so they have both their regular caregivers…"

"Oh, but of course. We have Mrs. Ballas's room all ready for her."

Constance bit her lip to keep her jaw from dropping. Luca was playing the Reverend Mother like a well-tuned violin. Good God, the man had no boundaries. He'd bribed a nun, no matter how he'd spun it.

"Excellent! Well, ladies, it's been a pleasure," he said, giving them a slight bow. "Darling, let's leave these saints to their work."

Constance let him take her hand and lead her from the office and back out onto the street before she pulled away. Luca glanced at her but kept walking. She had no choice but to trail after him.

"What was that?" she asked his retreating back.

"What?" He pulled his keys from his pocket, looking at her with genuine confusion.

"Laid it on a bit thick back there, didn't you?" she asked, folding her arms across her chest.

He shrugged. "I handled it. You've still got your position. We've got permission to have the kids stay, which will make the excursions—"

"Photo ops," she interjected.

"If that's how you prefer to see it."

"Of course that's how I prefer to see it. I always prefer to call a spade a spade."

"No," he said, coming back over to her. "You prefer to see the world as you want to see it and stubbornly refuse to see it any other way."

"Me? Stubborn? Looked in a mirror lately?"

The smile he gave her sent warm tingles rushing through her, and she looked away just to try and minimize his effect.

"As I've said, the children will be kept out of the photographers' way as much as possible. I can't guarantee no one will get a picture. But I can promise it won't be my doing and my team will do what we can to prevent it."

He sounded sincere enough. She hoped she could trust him. At least in this. "Thank you."

He nodded. "Let's get out of here," he said. "I've only had one cup of coffee and it wasn't nearly enough for being awake this early."

They'd reached his car. Joseph folded the paper he'd been reading and jumped out to open the back door for them.

Constance pulled out her keys. "I drove myself, remember?"

"Joseph will drive your scooter. You'll come with me."

She blew out an exasperated breath, trying not to lose her temper with the pompous ass. And failing. "That doesn't make any sense. I'm capable of driving myself. Besides, if he drives my scooter to my house, how will he get back home?"

Luca's eyes narrowed and a twinge of unease rattled Constance's stomach. He was obviously not used to being told no. Well, tough. She wasn't going to let him order her around.

He crowded into her personal space, stepping so close she had to crane her neck to meet his deep brown gaze. She tried to draw in a deep breath without giving away the fact she was suddenly finding it more difficult to breath. It was like the man was some inferno who absorbed all the oxygen around him and ignited anything female within a ten-mile radius. Constance had been around commanding, domineering men before. They all had the same swagger, the same presence. The whole *I'm king of the world and you will fear and obey me* mentality.

With Luca it was different. Oh, he had the ego and the charisma that most men of his station had, and he had more than his fair share of sex appeal, but he wasn't the first handsome, wealthy, powerful man she'd been around, or even been intimate with. Not that she'd been intimate with Luca, or ever would be. There was no reason this man should affect her this much. What the hell was it about him?

He stroked a hand down her arm, eliciting a tremble that left him giving her a smug smile and her glaring at him. Before she realized what he was doing, he'd plucked the keys from her hand and tossed them to Joseph. Constance started to give him a good chewing-out but he pressed a finger to her mouth.

"It isn't necessary to argue with everything I say." His finger brushed along her lips, igniting an instant fire that she wanted with all her being to give herself over to, but everything was happening too fast. He was too much, too overwhelming, and too overbearing by far.

She jerked back, but he just smiled. "Joseph needs to drive your moped because we have a little errand to run. He can bring it to my place and you can retrieve it there."

She frowned. "What errand? We've spoken with my director. I wasn't aware we had anything else planned for the day."

He sighed. "Ah, yes. It's all about you, isn't it?"

She planted her hands on her hips but he continued on

before she could get a word in. "We've seen your director, kept up my side of the bargain. You remain House Mother of the Year. Now it's your turn to help me with a little damage control. That was the agreement, correct?"

Her anger deflated a little and she dropped her arms. "Oh. Well, yes."

"Okay then. Joseph will take your scooter, and you'll come with me."

"Come with you where?" she asked, not trusting him one iota.

He cocked an eyebrow. "Are you always this difficult?"

"Are you always this bossy?"

"Generally, yes," he said with a smile that had probably charmed the panties off a thousand women. She tried to ignore the tingle it was inducing in her.

"I'll take good care of your…vehicle, ma'am," Joseph said.

"Thanks, Joseph."

He gave her a little bow and left them alone.

Luca gestured to his car. "We've got some shopping to do."

"Shopping?"

"Yes. You're my fiancée. You need to look the part. My jeweler is opening a little early so we can pick something out."

Her jaw dropped. "You're buying me a ring?"

# Chapter Four

Luca opened the car door but Constance remained frozen on the asphalt.

"Is something wrong?" he asked. He let his tone convey his irritation at her constant questioning of him but couldn't keep his amusement from showing along with it. He knew exactly what was wrong, and it was fun watching her squirm.

"I don't think it's necessary to get me a ring. This is a temporary thing, for show," she said, her pert little nose in the air.

"Exactly, and the second our engagement hits the newspapers the cameras are going to start zooming in on your finger. I don't want people thinking I'm cheap."

She couldn't seem to come up with an argument for that one. *Thank God.*

He went to open the door of his shiny silver Spyder 918, trying to rein in his impatience when he realized she hadn't followed him.

"Are you coming?"

She still hesitated. She'd agreed to the whole fake fiancée

thing, but it seemed like she might be having second thoughts. He couldn't really blame her there. He'd had nothing but second thoughts since Joe had suggested the crazy scheme to him. On the one hand, it would solve all his problems if they could pull it off. His father wasn't an idiot. He wasn't going to accept that his son had had an overnight change of heart. And the slew of doubts that had cropped up when he'd hopped in his car to get the whole charade started only multiplied when he'd shown up in her boss's office.

He knew his reasoning made sense. The director might not believe it was really him had he just called, and they might as well start being seen together. The sooner the better, in his mind. But Constance didn't seem to share his enthusiasm for getting a move on things, though she certainly hadn't complained when he'd been in front of her boss fixing her problems.

"What's wrong now?" he asked.

She shook her head, pink tingeing her cheeks. "I didn't expect things to start quite so soon. Or be quite so…elaborate."

His brow arched and she rolled her eyes. "Yeah, I know that doesn't make any sense."

Luca sighed and came over to her, standing close enough she had to crane her neck to meet his eyes. God, she seemed so tiny. If she looked straight ahead, as she did now instead of meeting his eyes, she had a great view of the base of his throat. He hoped she enjoyed it, as there were much more appealing views he could offer her if she'd just unclench a little bit. No reason they couldn't have a little fun while playing their parts. In fact, it would help the whole authentic angle greatly. However, as he was currently having trouble even getting her to let him buy her jewelry, getting to do anything more intimate was going to take a lot more effort on his part.

He gazed down at her. "Are we still going? Or have you changed your mind?"

She looked up, her eyes meeting his, and took a deep breath. "I don't know if I can do this."

A slight frown furrowed his brow. "What?"

"This," she said, waving her hand between them. "I don't even know you and I'm supposed to pretend like we're engaged. You're a stranger to me. How do I convince anyone we're...we're..."

"In love? Getting married? Intimate?" he said, his voice deepening on that last one.

Constance glared up at him, which did nothing but spark an amused grin.

"Yes," she hissed. "All of that."

"Well," he said, reaching out to draw her resisting body into his arms, "the best way to get over a case of nerves is to jump in with both feet."

He cupped the back of her neck and captured her lips before she could open her mouth to protest. She resisted... for all of a half a second before her body softened and she sank into his kiss. He pulled her in closer, his head slanting to get a better angle. He'd only meant to steal a quick kiss, a little demonstration, but the moment his lips touched hers all thoughts of anything but the woman in his arms evaporated.

Up close, the faint cherry blossom fragrance of her hair filled his senses, forever marking that scent as hers. Her soft lips fit against his perfectly, like they were made just for him. His head buzzed when her hands slid up his chest, leaving a trail of fire tingling in their wake. Good God, if this is how it felt kissing her when she was pretending not to enjoy it, how would it be if she truly gave in and let herself savor the passion he could sense running through her? The delightful Stanzia was a volcano long overdue for an explosion. She just didn't realize it yet. He couldn't wait to enlighten her.

Her lips opened under his, her teeth grazing his bottom lip...before they sank in deep.

He jerked his head away, but grasped her hands to prevent her from shoving him completely away. The pain snapped him out of whatever haze he'd been in. He'd never, ever forgotten where he was and who was watching before. Oh sure, he didn't give a flying shit most of the time, but that didn't mean he wasn't aware of it, until he'd tasted those sweet lips of hers. The prim Miss McMurty was dangerous.

He tightened his grip on her hands when she tried to pull away, keeping her close and twisting his body so any view of her from the street was shielded.

He licked his lip to take some of the sting away. "Now, that wasn't very nice." The intention behind it, maybe. The actual experience of it had been fucking hot. He'd give a large chunk of his fortune to have her bite him again. In private so he could really enjoy it. And return the favor.

She glared at him. "You can't kiss me whenever you want!"

"Yes," he said, leaning back over her. "I can. You're my fiancée, Stanzia. That means people expect us to act a certain way. I believe kissing one's fiancée is perfectly reasonable behavior."

"My name is Constance. And yes, when we're in public is one thing," she said, her beautiful blue eyes spitting fire. "We aren't in public right now. I mean, not really. Standing on the street doesn't count."

She had no clue how much scrutiny he was under. Always. Luca sighed and hugged her to him so he could whisper in her ear. "Across the street, in the bushes."

She glanced up at him, her forehead creased in confusion. He turned them slightly so she could look in the direction he'd indicated. Her little gasp let him know she'd seen what he'd spotted the second he'd arrived. A man camped out in the bushes, his camera poised and ready.

"When you're with me, it's always public," he said, hating

the note of sad resignation he heard in his own voice.

The constant media attention had been fun at first, when he was young and stupid and wanted to be famous. The older he'd gotten, the less fun it had become. They captured everything, not just the moments he was dressed to the nines and ready to strut his stuff, but *everything*. Him staggering outside a club. Him stopping in for a coffee. Him walking across his private beach the morning after getting his heart broken. Someone had even snapped a picture of him in his own shower. He'd had to fire his entire staff after that one because he couldn't find out who did it and no one would confess. Now his only live-in help were Joe and Mrs. Lasko, his housekeeper, a sweet old woman who was one of the few people on the planet he trusted. The cleaning staff came in a few times a week.

He hated it, but it was his life now. He was used to it. Constance wasn't. And the guilt that jabbed at him every time he thought of dragging this sweet, innocent woman into his world was nearly enough for him to call the whole thing off. Nearly. But he needed her too badly, and she only had to deal with it for six weeks. Then she could go back to her anonymous life. The paparazzi might hound her for a little while afterward, but they'd move on soon enough. She'd get to escape. He wouldn't be so lucky. None of it would matter if they didn't pull this off. He needed her on board. Now.

She gazed up at him, the anger gone from her features. "I didn't think it would start so soon," she murmured.

He brushed a thumb across her cheek. "We only have a month to convince my father I've changed. And we need to convince your director you aren't some sex-crazed, celebrity-obsessed nut job, in case they don't feel like taking my word for it."

She glared at him again for that one and he grinned back at her. "Which means," he said, "you need to get into your new fiancé's car and get a move on. It would be really nice if you didn't attack me every time I try and touch you."

She snorted and his grin grew wider at such an undignified sound coming from his little schoolmarm.

"I'm not making any promises," she said.

That had him laughing outright. He kissed her again, turning his body to give the photographer a better angle, and then released her.

"Did he get a good enough shot or should we go at it right here on the hood of your car?" she asked. Her tone was deceptively sweet, but the fire was back in her eyes.

Luca pressed her against the passenger door, his lips against her ear while his hands trailed up her sides as close as he dared to the bountiful offering her breasts presented. "Baby, we can go at it anywhere you want. You just say the word."

Her mouth dropped open but before she could slap him as he rightly deserved, he stepped back.

Her eyes shot daggers at him. "I wouldn't want to damage the paint job. What is with this car, anyway? For someone who acts like he doesn't want attention, you're sure going about not getting it the wrong way. You could buy your own island for what you probably spent on this thing. You don't even really need a car here."

"It's pretty. Leave my toys alone," he said, opening the door for her. "Are you coming?" He pointed to the passenger seat.

She rolled her eyes, but she got in the car, slamming the door rather harder than necessary.

Luca didn't have to fake the smile on his face as he moved around to the driver's side. Constance might wear the prim and proper schoolteacher façade like a coat of armor, but beneath it was a hellcat waiting to be unleashed. The little glimpses he'd already seen fired him up like no one he'd ever met before. Then again, the thought of her kids entering the picture put a serious damper on things. His life wasn't built for kids. Even if it was, he was definitely not father material. Never had been and never would be.

He just hoped it was all worth it, because as appealing as Constance was, having to deal with her kids terrified him to no end.

# Chapter Five

"I can't go ring shopping yet."

Luca rubbed his temples. "This must be what an aneurysm feels like."

"Oh, stop being so dramatic. You're worse than my girls."

His mouth dropped open but before he could respond to that little barb, she continued. "I have to go meet with my father. He made a trip to the island especially to meet with me. I need to fill him in on all of…this," she said, waving her hand between them. "He's already determined to ship me back to the States after seeing the pictures from last night. I'm not looking forward to telling him what's come of it, but I'd like to tell him what's going on before he sees more pictures of me in the magazines, only this time sporting some huge shiny ring."

"We've gone from not wanting a ring to want something huge and shiny, huh?"

She shrugged. "Not at all. I just figured that would be the direction you'd be gravitating to."

He didn't really want to point out the obvious, but he needed to make sure she was completely on board with the whole plan. "You can't tell him the truth."

Her mouth pursed in a thin line. "I'm aware of that, and believe me, as much as I hate lying to my father, the last thing I want to do is tell him the truth about this mess. We might not be all that close these days, but he's my father. I can't just get engaged and not tell him."

He frowned, wondering what the deal was between her and her dad. Before he could say anything she blew out an exasperated breath. "He has a demanding job. I have six kids he didn't entirely approve of me signing up for. We're busy people so we don't talk much. But still…"

He gave her a sharp nod. "Yeah, I understand. All right, then. We'll go to brunch with your father and then we'll go shopping."

"Wait, what? No. You don't need to come."

His eyebrow raised. Did he detect a note of panic in her voice? "What's the matter? You don't want your dad to meet me? Isn't it customary for the fiancé to meet the father? In fact, I should probably ask his permission, shouldn't I?"

She paled and her eyes grew wide. "Please don't even joke about that."

Luca frowned. He'd been playing with her a bit, yes. But she seemed genuinely upset by the idea that he meet her dad, and that seemed odd. And a bit insulting. "Why don't you want me to meet him? Is he really going to be that angry? Are you afraid of him?"

"What? No, of course not."

"Well, then what is it? I'm not going to send you in there alone if he's going to be upsetting you."

The surprise on her face softened and she laughed and shook her head. "I'm…flattered you're concerned for me. But I'll be fine, really. It's just not every day a girl has to sit down and explain a bunch of pictures that are splattered all over the internet and then tell her dad that she's engaged to a rather famous…person…such as yourself…" Her cheeks flamed. As well they should.

He choked back the first few responses that came to mind. He couldn't really blame her for not wanting to tell her dad about him. He didn't have the best reputation. And he was blackmailing her, after all.

"Fine. If you are certain you'll be okay…"

"I'm sure."

He nodded and glanced down at his watch. "All right. I've got something I want to do anyway. I'll drop you off and then come back for you in…an hour?"

"Make it half an hour. I don't think this'll take long and I don't want to stick around too long once I tell him."

He let his gaze roam over her again, surprised that she was so rattled. Any man who could make the formidable Miss McMurty squirm was someone he'd like to meet. Another day. When his daughter wasn't about to tell him she was marrying a stranger who was a famous party animal. Best to just let her handle that part. Cowardly or not, he had no desire to be skewered by a ferocious Papa Bear.

"Half hour then." That would give him enough time to grab a few things and be back to get her. Hopefully when he returned she'd actually be waiting for him and it wasn't all some ploy to ask her father for asylum from her big, bad, would-be fiancé.

Constance took another sip of her water and waited for her father to say something. He seemed…stunned was probably the only word for it.

"I'm not sure I'm understanding this," he said, folding his napkin and placing it on the table. That was never a good sign. "When we spoke last night you assured me nothing was going on, that what appeared to be happening in those pictures wasn't the true story and that you didn't know this man at all and it was all a strange coincidence. And now, you're telling me that you are marrying this man?"

"Yes?"

"Is that a question?"

Constance took a deep breath. She was a strong, independent woman, raising six kids. And still her father's disapproval made her cringe, but there was no help for it. Might as well just get it over with.

"No, it's not a question. Yes, I am marrying him. I… haven't been entirely truthful with you." She'd remain vague on exactly which parts she wasn't being honest on. His frown deepened. "That much is obvious."

She knew he had every right to be upset, but it was beginning to wear on her, and Luca would be back any minute. She needed this uncomfortable meeting over with so she could go on to an even more uncomfortable one. She sighed. How had her life gotten so unbelievably out of control in so short a time?

"I don't want to get into all the details. For now, all you need to know is that he's a good man who I've agreed to marry and I didn't want you to find out by reading the papers."

"I'd say the 'good man' part was debatable. I'm aware of who he is, the stories about him."

"You can't believe everything you read," she said. At least that part was true enough. "You don't know him."

"You're right, I don't." He sat back and folded his hands across his still-trim stomach. "You're supposedly marrying this man I've never met. Wouldn't the respectful thing to do be to come to me and ask my permission?"

Constance's eyebrow rose at that. "Dad, I haven't asked your permission to do anything since I was fourteen years old and enrolled myself in boarding school."

His mouth quirked up at the corners in a small smile. "Well, that's true enough. You always did follow your own mind. Shipping yourself off to boarding school. Trading in that two-month cruise around the world I got you for a graduation present to go backpacking through Europe with those crazy friends of yours. Staying out here and getting involved in that program with all those kids when you'd only come out for a vacation to visit me." He shook his head. "You are so much like your mother."

Constance answered his fondly sad smile with one of her own. "Oh, I don't know. The adventurous side I might get from her. The independent, stubborn side is all you."

He laughed and Constance relaxed into her chair. He might not be thrilled with the situation—hell, who was? But he wouldn't make an issue out of it. For the moment.

He glanced down at his watch. "I'm afraid I've got to be going." He signaled the server and handed over his credit card to pay for their drinks. The young man returned quickly with his card and her father stood and held out his arms. She savored the hug. He wasn't a demonstrative man, but she knew he loved her.

"I'll trust that you know what you're doing," he said, giving her one last squeeze before letting her go. "And that you'll let me know if you need anything."

"I will," she said, almost limp with relief that the meeting was over. Now, if she could get him out of there before Luca showed up. She had no desire for the two men to meet.

"Good." He gave her a quick kiss on the forehead. "Because if he doesn't treat you right, I know people. Keep that in mind."

Constance laughed at that and shook her head as he walked away, and not a moment too soon. Luca's car pulled up to the door just as she stepped outside. Say what you will about him, but the man had impeccable timing.

He jumped out and hurried around to get the door for her, pulling her in for a quick kiss before she could get inside.

"Quit doing that," she muttered.

"Not a chance. It's the best perk of this whole situation and I have every intention of taking advantage of it."

He stepped away from the door and she slipped inside as quickly as she could.

Constance settled back against the leather seat of Luca's car, her heart still pounding furiously, and not from the realization that there had been a photographer hidden in the bushes earlier, or that she'd just told her father, and everyone else important in her life, that she was getting married. She licked her lips, letting her teeth lightly scrape along the flesh that still tingled from where he'd kissed her. Her heart was trying to jump out of her chest because of *him*.

She'd wondered what it would be like to kiss him. Just getting close the first time they'd met had swept her up so much she'd almost forgotten herself, which was exactly what had gotten her into this whole mess in the first place. She didn't know what it was about him. Yeah, sure the man was chiseled like he'd been carved from solid marble and exuded sex like some kind of walking pheromone. But a simple kiss, even from a walking wet dream like Luca, shouldn't totally eradicate twenty-seven years of strict upbringing. It was all well and good to be passionate in the bedroom, but somehow the man had reduced her to making out in the streets like some hormonal tart. What was truly terrifying was she didn't even think he was trying. Heaven help her if he put any real effort into seducing her.

Constance inwardly rolled her eyes at herself at the tart thought, wishing she could get rid of her grandmother's voice scolding her in her own head. Still, the thought stood. Supreme example of a male specimen or not, she should have better control over herself. Maybe it was because he kept catching her unawares. Both the near and actual kisses had been ambush jobs, sprung on her when she wasn't expecting it. Surely, if she knew they were coming she'd be able to keep a bit more composure about her.

He hopped in his side and glanced at her over the rim of his sunglasses. "So? How did it go?"

"As well as can be expected," she said.

"Excellent. Here." He reached to the backseat and came back with what looked like a shoebox. "I got you something."

"What is this?"

He pulled the car away from the restaurant and out onto the main road. "Open it and find out."

She wasn't sure if she should be afraid or excited by that exuberant lilt in his voice. She opened the box. She still wasn't sure how to feel. Inside lay the cutest pair of gold sandals with a little strap that went around the ankle. They looked like something she'd have worn before she had six kids and focused more on comfort than fashion.

"Luca…I don't know what to say…"

"Do you like them?"

He actually sounded like he was worried she might not.

"I love them. But…"

"Nope. No buts. The saleswoman assured me they are so comfortable you'll think you're walking on clouds. Or some nonsense like that."

"Thank you," she said, not sure if she should say anything else. She'd never had a man buy her shoes before.

He nodded. "There's several more pairs in the trunk, along with some other clothes."

"What?" she said, her gratitude quickly evaporating.

He shrugged. "If you're going to be my fiancée you need to dress the part."

"What's wrong with the way I dress?"

He looked her up and down before turning his gaze back

to the road. "You're not completely hopeless."

"Gee, thanks."

"Except for those shoes of yours. Try on the new ones."

She had a good mind to take one and smack him upside the head with it, but the leather was deliciously soft and her old sandals were about ready to fall apart. Wouldn't hurt to try them. She slid them on her feet and had to bite her lip to keep from groaning. Walking on a cloud indeed. The whole charade might be worth it just for those shoes.

"We'll be at the shop soon. Ready?"

She stared into those deep brown eyes of his, the faint hazelnut taste of him still on her lips, and took a shuddering breath. "Not really, but it's not going to get any better with waiting. Let's get this over with."

"Most women are a little more excited at the prospect of jewelry."

Constance crossed her arms, fully aware she was pouting and not caring at all. "It seems wrong. It's not like a little pair of earrings or something."

"You'd prefer earrings?"

She groaned. "That's not what I meant."

His lips twitched and her eyes narrowed. He was having entirely too much fun at her expense.

"Then what did you mean?" he asked.

"A diamond ring is expensive, even a small one. It's a waste of money and completely unnecessary."

"First of all, it's very necessary. People will expect you to be flashing some serious bling. And secondly, don't worry about the money. I've got plenty of it."

"You don't say," she said, drily.

"Sell the damn thing when we're done and give the money to some charity if it'll make you feel better, but you're getting a ring."

She mulled that over for a second. It wasn't a bad idea

and did actually ease her mind about the whole thing. If he was going to insist on spending the money, she might as well put it to good use.

"All right then. I will."

He shook his head, but let the matter drop. And thankfully, he didn't discuss the whole kissing episode either. She supposed she had a great deal more of that to look forward to. Although *dread* was probably a better word, and she'd keep telling herself that. Maybe she'd believe it. Either way, she needed to make sure she kept a handle on things. She had her girls to think about. They were all that mattered and she needed to make sure that nothing that was about to happen would negatively affect them in any way. They needed to come first, no matter what.

Luca eased out onto the road. Once he'd navigated through the narrowest of the streets, he held out a hand. She glanced at it, then him, completely confused.

He blew out an exasperated breath. "Take my hand, Stanzia."

"Stop calling me that. My name is Constance."

"Why do you dislike me calling you Stanzia so much?"

She didn't. That was the problem. She'd never had a nickname before. She'd always been Constance, even when she was little. Beyond the novelty of it, having the soft sounds of his pet name for her rolling off his tongue made things ache inside that she didn't want to examine too closely. She could imagine him whispering that name to her in the dark all too well. It was melodic and exotic and unique, and she was none of those things. But when he used that name, she felt like she was, and with him maybe she could be. But then what? Then she'd go back to her real life and Stanzia would be gone. She'd be Constance again. Better to remain Constance. Keep that layer of distance between them that the pet name shattered.

When she didn't answer, he just shook his head and stuck

his hand out again. "Take my hand."

She frowned. The thought of holding his hand sent a warm ball of fuzzies spreading through her. Her fingers itched to curl around his; all the more reason to resist.

"What for?"

He briefly glanced at her, then back out the windshield. "Because you jump ten feet every time I get anywhere near you. We need to get used to each other and practice makes perfect, as they say."

She still looked at his offered hand like it was a bomb ready to go off. It might not be in the literal sense, but voluntarily letting him touch her in any way was just another sexual accident waiting to happen.

"Stanzia. Do you want this little charade to work or not? Take my hand."

She sighed, knowing full well she was being ridiculous. Holding hands. It was a small enough thing to do.

"Fine," she said, slipping her hand into his. She couldn't stop the little shiver of pleasure that skated up her spine as his warm skin slid across hers.

He laced their fingers together and turned his attention back to the road, although his thumb lazily caressed the back of her hand. It was such a sweet gesture, intimate even. She resisted the urge to squirm and focused her attention on the gorgeous island scenery flowing past her window. After a few minutes she began to relax, the rhythmic stroking of his thumb becoming almost soothing, or at least it would have been had the thumb doing the stroking belonged to anyone other than Luca.

"So," he said, startling her out of her momentary comfort zone. "How long have you lived on the island?"

Her gut reaction was to tell him to mind his own business, but she supposed they did need to get to know each other a little. "About five years."

"What brought you out here?"

"My father worked at the embassy in Athens. I came out with him from New York and fell in love with it. Mykonos was always my favorite. I always meant to go back home, but then I started helping out with the Family Aid groups and decided to make things permanent."

He shook his head. "You just made things permanent? Took on six children for the rest of your life on a whim?"

"I didn't say it was on a whim. I didn't come to the decision lightly. But they needed me. I'd been helping in the house Sophia, Magdalena, Callie, and Elena were in, so they knew me. Trusted me. And I already loved them. Their House Mother fell ill and wasn't going to be able to continue caring for them. There were no other homes available that could take so many. If I hadn't stepped up, Sophia, Magdalena, and Callie might have been split up. I couldn't let that happen. With Lexi and Irene, it was the same thing. And Elena…" Her smile grew a bit sad. "I already had more kids than I'd meant to take on, but she doesn't trust many people. Won't even speak to most people. We formed a bond, somehow. I figured she was meant to be with me."

He nodded, but a small crease in his forehead suggested he couldn't quite understand her choices. She didn't expect someone like him to understand so it was hardly surprising.

"Aren't you curious about where I live when I'm not here? What I do?" he asked.

Constance shrugged. "I don't read the tabloids, of course, but I've heard enough of the gossip to know most of it, I think."

Luca's face hardened. "You shouldn't believe everything you hear," he said, his voice low and gruff. "Those so-called journalists don't know anything about me."

She searched his face, hoping for a hint as to what he was really thinking. She couldn't possibly have hurt his feelings.

Could she? Shame tugged at her. Despite his playboy reputation—and nothing she'd seen so far had suggested the gossip about Luca was anything but true—even a man like him must have feelings. Whether the stories she'd heard were true or not, it must suck to have people assume they knew everything about you when they didn't even know you.

"You're right. I apologize," she said.

He glanced at her, a bit surprised, but waved it off. "Don't worry about it."

"So, spill it then. I know you don't live here full time, and I can't imagine that even half the stories I've heard can be true. So what do you do when you're not in Greece?"

Luca's body relaxed and the tension level in the car decreased.

"I'm in New York frequently, so we have that in common. And if all this works and I start running the New York offices I suppose I'll spend most of my time there."

She'd known that much. She'd seen the pictures to prove how much he enjoyed the nightlife the city offered. But she kept her mouth shut and let him talk.

"I try to come here a few times a year. It's quieter but still offers more than enough entertainment, and even with paparazzi roaming around, it's still not as bad as back in the States. Usually. I'm afraid our little escapade yesterday might have stirred up the hornets a bit."

"To put it mildly," Constance said, letting the sarcasm liberally soak her words.

"Anyway," he said, the eye roll evident in his tone, "my family is in real estate. I guess I don't spend as much time at the office as my father would like."

"Do you spend *any* time there?"

Luca scowled at her and Constance braced herself against the natural inclination to cringe.

"I keep abreast of what's going on. My father has always

had everything under control. He doesn't need me there."

Before Constance could dig at that particular can of worms, Luca turned down a narrow lane and weaved the car through several more streets before finally pulling to a stop in front of a jewelry store set in among the other shops on a typical brightly colored street. This shop was definitely more upscale than the rest. The façade looked carved from marble with double glass doors instead of the whitewashed stone and bright blue or red painted wood doors of the surrounding shops. Her stomach bottomed out. She couldn't go in there. What had they been thinking? She couldn't be engaged… especially to someone like him. She was so ordinary and he was the playboy prince of the Mediterranean.

Luca got out and walked to her side, opening her door. When she didn't get out he poked his head inside, getting way too up close and personal. She tried to sit back farther but was already up against the seat. His gaze dropped to her bare legs and lingered for several moments before looking back at her face. His smile nearly stole her breath away.

"Coming?"

That sent all sorts of inappropriate thoughts flying through her head. She'd never survive six weeks of him. "You know this is crazy, right?" she said to try and excuse her suddenly heated cheeks and short breath. "No one is going to believe it."

Luca took her hand and tugged her from the car. "Of course they will. Your boss didn't seem to suspect anything. I don't see why anyone else would."

"Everyone will believe you because you tell them to?"

"Yes."

She shook her head. "You really are arrogant, you know that?"

He shrugged. "Is it arrogance if it's true?" Then he frowned. "Why are you so convinced no one will buy this?"

Was he really going to make her say it? He stared at her, waiting for an answer. Apparently he was.

"I'm not the type of woman you usually date."

That amused grin was back. "What type of woman do I usually date?"

Constance did roll her eyes at that one. "Supermodels. Actresses. Tall, thin, gorgeous women with legs up to their necks and paparazzi of their own. I'm attractive enough, I guess, but I'm hardly who people will expect you to be marrying."

Luca helped her from the car but instead of stepping back, he pulled her into his arms. She pulled against him a little, noticing the people beginning to stare. His car was impossible to miss. And so was Luca. People were starting to point and whip out their cell phones.

"Everyone is watching."

He held on tighter. "Good. That's the point. You need to learn to ignore them. Pretend they aren't there. Unless they are right in your face, it's not too hard. The tourists will keep back."

"I thought you were against PDA."

"I am, when it's for real. But we want to put on a show, remember?"

Her eyes still darted back and forth until he captured her face in his hands and forced her to look at him.

"Ignore them." He leaned in and kissed her until her mind fogged and she couldn't remember what she was nervous about. When he pulled away, she remained passive in his arms. Was sedation by seduction possible?

"Now that I have your attention," he said, smiling down at her like he was perfectly aware of his effect. "You are more than just 'attractive enough' and I would be happy to demonstrate how beautiful I think you are any time you want. I've never given a fuck what other people think and I have no intention of starting now. However, it would help matters if you'd stop acting like this was a sham and start acting the part."

He pressed a gentle kiss to her lips and instead of jerking away she let herself enjoy the sensation of his lips moving over hers. It was over all too soon. He pulled away and took her hand again.

"For the next six weeks, Stanzia, you are mine. Don't forget it."

Oh she wouldn't. It was all she *could* think about. But what happened once their time was up? He'd already stirred desires she had no time or energy to deal with, and she had no room for that kind of male-induced drama in her life. No price was too high to pay to keep her girls with her.

But spending six weeks with Luca might be dangerously close.

# Chapter Six

Luca watched Constance's eyes widen until her eyebrows nearly hit her hairline as the selection of rings was presented. The jeweler kept placing massive ring upon massive ring in front of her, clearly aware of Luca's ability to pony up the cash and determined to make the biggest sale possible. Constance, however, wasn't making the job easy. She waved off every gaudy monstrosity the jeweler tried to put on her finger. A fine sheen of sweat formed on the man's brow, probably at the prospect that she wouldn't find anything to her liking and he'd lose an enormous sale.

"Well, what would madam prefer?" the jeweler finally asked.

"I…" Constance glanced at Luca, clearly pleading for help.

He took pity on her. It was impossible not to with those eyes of hers gazing up at him like a puppy begging for treats.

"Perhaps something a little simpler," he said.

He was immediately rewarded with a relieved smile.

"Yes," she agreed. "Something simple."

The jeweler's forehead creased in a minute frown but he produced a tray of solitaires; simple, yet each large enough to cover her finger from base to knuckle. Constance chewed on her bottom lip, her eyes roaming over the selection.

Luca spied a ring tucked in among a display of sapphires and leaned down for a closer look. The center stone was a decent sized, probably three carats or so, a square-cut sapphire that shined with deep-blue fire under the lights. It was surrounded by small diamonds with another round sapphire nestled beside them on each side, set in a simple platinum band.

"That one," he said, pointing to it. "Let's see that one."

Constance glanced at him in surprise and then down at the ring that they handed to him. Her face softened, a small sigh escaping her lips. He took her hand and slid the ring on her left ring finger.

"Luca, it's beautiful," she said, gazing down at it.

He brought her hand up to his lips, his eyes locking with hers as he pressed a kiss to the ring on her finger. "It's not as beautiful as those big blue eyes of yours, but it's close," he said, loving the blush that stained her cheeks.

He'd said the words to keep up his part in the charade, but the moment he said them, he realized he meant every word. Instead of exploring that concerning thought, he turned back to the jeweler. "I think we'll take this one."

"Very good, sir," he said.

Luca let go of Constance long enough to take care of the details and then rejoined her. He caught her staring at the ring, holding it up to let the light shine through and spread blue-tinged rainbows throughout the room. A smile touched his lips before he recognized the emotion gently warming him. He'd felt a range of things for the women in his life over the years. Lust, certainly. Protectiveness, sometimes. Affection, occasionally. Love, not to any significant degree, but tenderness…never. Until now.

He didn't know what it was about her. Maybe it was because she despised him, or acted like she did. It was a novel experience being loathed by a woman. Or maybe it was that the things that mattered so much to everyone else in his life meant nothing to her. She didn't care about his money, fame, fancy cars, or famous friends. That stuff made her want him less, not more. She might spend most of their conversations criticizing him and his lifestyle, but at least when she spoke he knew it was the real her speaking, not some version of her she thought he might like. There were few genuine people in his life—Joe, his housekeeper Mrs. Lasko, his father, and now Constance.

Before he could reflect too deeply on the bombardment of unwelcome feelings trying to creep their way into his heart, dozens of blinding lights flashed through the window. Constance jumped, a hand covering her mouth to try and contain the startled squeak that he heard anyway.

Luca sighed. Time to get the show on the road.

He slipped an arm around her waist and pulled her close, pressing a kiss to her temple to keep the hovering jeweler from overhearing. "When we go out we'll walk straight to my car. I'll open the door for you. Please don't fight me on it. It'll just leave you in the middle of the vultures for longer, but make sure they get a good shot of the ring."

Her panicked expression melted into annoyance. Her lips might have been smiling but her eyes were shooting daggers. "How do I do that?"

Anger was good. Anger didn't make him want to cuddle up with her on some overstuffed couch and watch old movies in their fuzzy pajamas. And anger would serve her better navigating through the circus that was his life than her sweet, gentle side would.

"Let your hand dangle. Don't put it in your pocket. Shade

your eyes from the cameras with that hand. We're in a jewelry store after being caught making out at my home. Joe's been helping the rumors fly. They'll be trying to get shots of your left hand anyway so all you have to do is not impede them. They're pretty good at getting what they want."

He knew his bitterness was leaking out but he couldn't help it. Constance's anger faded a bit, replaced by a soft contemplation he wasn't sure how to deal with.

The store's manager escorted them to the door along with two men in security uniforms. "Our security officers will help get you to your vehicle, sir."

Luca nodded. "Thank you." Joe usually helped run interference for him when necessary but Luca had underestimated the need for such measures for their little shopping excursion. Oh, he'd known the photogs would be there, definitely, but not crowding so thickly around the doors that they wouldn't be able to get out. "Ready?"

She took a deep breath and nodded, looping her arm around his waist so she could shelter under his shoulder. The manager opened the door and the first security guard began pushing his way through the crowd. The other would follow behind them, guarding their backs. Luca got a firmer grip on Constance's waist and led her into the mob.

Her hand fisted in his shirt and she ducked her head, curling against him as much as she could and still walk. She raised her hand to shield her face from the cameras and the blinding flashes going off. The lights shone off her new engagement ring and the air rang with shouted questions.

Luca didn't know if she was trying to show off the ring as he'd asked or if she was genuinely trying to hide her face from the cameras and had just forgotten her new accessory. Either way, the photographers were getting more than their fair share of pictures. By the end of the day there would probably be photos on every available publication and social media site out there. Mission accomplished. He should be happy; instead, he was pissed.

He opened the passenger door to his car and ushered Constance inside as fast as he could, slamming the door behind her so he could run around to the other side. The second he was in the car he cranked the engine and revved the gas, giving the paparazzi vultures a very brief warning he was about to move. If they chose not to get out of the way that was their fault. Unfortunately, they all moved enough they didn't get run over and he was able to pull out on the street. Constance looked at him with wide eyes.

"Is it always like that?"

Luca gritted his teeth so hard his jaw ached, then forced himself to relax. "No. Not always. Hopefully it'll die down a bit now that they've got some shots of you with the ring. That'll give them a few juicy details to splash around for a little while. And since we are planning on some photo ops, they might agree to leave us alone for the most part. There are always a few that will follow no matter what, but some of them aren't too bad and will back off as long as they get an opportunity to get a good shot another time."

"Yeah, well those few who will follow no matter what are on our tail."

Luca looked into the rear view mirror and swore. "Hold on."

• • •

Constance grabbed the door frame and tried to keep from shrieking as Luca suddenly swerved to the right, taking a corner he'd already nearly passed. The car made it with a squeal of tires and he gunned it.

"Aren't you going a little fast?" she asked.

"Only way to lose them."

"Are you nuts? You can't lose them. This isn't some car chase movie."

Luca snorted. "Look behind us, Stanzia. It's exactly what it is. Don't worry. I know what I'm doing."

She bit back another scream of terror as he zoomed up another narrow street. "Luca, this is insane. Slow down!"

"I've done this a million times."

He cranked the wheel again and she braced herself to keep from being thrown against the car door. "You're going to get us both killed!"

"Hasn't anyone ever told you not to distract the driver?"

"You're enjoying this!"

The grin he turned on her blazed with excitement. But there was something else there, behind his eyes. Something she couldn't name but that seemed inexorably sad. Before she could dwell on it too long, he made another right into one of the few parking lots on the island, zooming down one of the aisles until he came to an empty spot. He swerved in and cut the engine.

Seconds later, the three paparazzo on scooters whizzed by the lot, not even pausing.

"There," Luca said with a smile. "Lost them."

Constance straightened from where she'd been cringing against the door and slapped his arm. "The next time you want to risk your life driving a hundred miles an hour through town, you let me out of the car first! What the hell were you thinking?"

His eyebrow rose at that, but his smile just grew broader. "I was thinking I'd give the bastards the slip. And I did. How about a little gratitude?"

"Gratitude? Are you kidding? We could have been killed. I've got kids! If you want to throw your life away, be my guest, but my life is spoken for. My girls have been through enough without losing another parent, thank you very much."

Luca waved her off. "You're being dramatic."

"No, I'm not." She yanked on her seat belt to get it off her neck.

"It's no big deal, Constance. They were chasing us. Now they're not. End of story."

She opened her mouth to object again. Her heart still pounded so hard she was probably going to have internal bruising and if she didn't catch her breath soon she was going to hyperventilate. She focused on drawing a few deep breaths in and out of her lungs.

A man, presumably the owner or person who worked at the lot, ran toward them, his face a mottled purple as he chewed them out in rapid Greek. Luca rolled down his window, apologized, and slapped a large wad of euros in the man's hand. He rolled the window back up while the man was still smiling and inviting him to stay longer.

Constance still hadn't regained full control of herself but Luca completely ignored her borderline panic attack and moved on. "I was going to take you home to grab whatever you'll need for the next few weeks, but we need to get back. I think Joe has something planned with the kids this afternoon."

"I don't live too far from here. It wouldn't take long to swing by."

She told him the address and he checked his watch. "All right, but we'll need to hurry. Joe will get his panties in a bunch if we ruin his plans."

"What about the girls' things?"

"We can deal with moving them over tomorrow. I think the first night we should be on our own. Get that woman who helps you to watch them. They'll survive without you for one night."

Constance shook her head, the whole situation beginning to feel like a giant wave that was getting ready to slam into her and drag her under. How did she go from a quiet House

Mother to being chased by the paparazzi? Somehow it didn't seem possible that it had just been yesterday that she'd collected the girls to go for a walk that had led her into this man's yard. And arms. And bed if he had his way.

Oh, she hadn't forgotten that little nugget of sheer insanity, and now she had a massive rock on her finger that weighed her down, dragging her under the wave of emotions it was getting harder to contain.

"Before that happens, we need to discuss—"

"There's nothing left to discuss," he said, impatiently, restarting the car and easing out of the parking lot.

"You don't know even know what I'm going to say."

"I know exactly what you're going to say. You had no idea it was going to be like this. It's too much. You don't think you can deal with it all. It's not worth it." His hands gripped the steering wheel until his knuckles turned white, but he kept his gaze firmly on the road. "Save it. I've heard it before. My charming personality isn't the only reason I'm single. You, however, have signed an ironclad contract. I held up my end. You are still in your director's good graces. Your turn to hold up your end."

Constance bit her lip. Oh, he'd definitely heard it all before. His tone was so bitter she had no doubt whoever had said it had hurt him badly, perhaps several someones. It couldn't be an easy life to live. Despite his domineering manner and the terrifying encounter they'd just had, along with the promise of future daily torments, Constance didn't want to be the next person to give him the same speech. Even if she'd been ready to do just that.

She sat straighter in her seat, mentally re-gathering her wits. "That's not what I was going to say," she said quietly.

"No?" he asked with a mild scowl, obviously not believing the lie.

Fine. He didn't have to believe it. It didn't matter anyhow.

"No," she repeated. "I was, however, going to say that if this is what your life is always like, I'm not sure I can condone the children's participation in all this."

Luca's frown deepened. "The children were Joe's idea. I don't necessarily disagree with you. I certainly wouldn't want my own children subjected to this shit day in and day out. Which is why I'm never going to have any. But in this instance at least, I can assure you they'll be fine. Joe has arranged for some private excursions somewhere and has invited specific photographers. Not those paparazzi vultures that follow me around. We'll have enough security there no one will get near them. The photographers will only be there for a few minutes for some shots of us. We'll keep the kids out of sight. They won't be swarmed, and they'll be safer on my estate than in your house at the moment. It won't be hard for the press to find out where you live. At least at my place the gates will keep them out."

Constance hesitated. Part of her wanted to delve into what he'd said. Deciding not to have children because you didn't want them stalked by photographers was a special kind of depressing. She could understand to a degree. For someone like her who craved security and organization, the chaos and constant danger created by always being hounded would drive her insane. At the same time, how unutterably sad that the fame that made this man so sought after was also what might keep him alone for the rest of his life. However, the larger, more cautious part of her knew he wouldn't welcome her commentary on the matter. So, for the moment anyway, she'd keep her mouth shut and focus on the children in her care.

"I guess that makes sense… I suppose if you can guarantee their safety…"

"I've already said I can."

She nodded and let the matter drop. They pulled to a stop

in front of her modest home and Luca jumped out. Constance opened her door before he could but he took her hand and helped her out, his eyes briefly scanning the bushes across the street from her house.

She looked over her shoulder, dismay filling her. "You think they're here, too?"

"Probably," he muttered. "Let's get inside."

She didn't waste any more time asking questions but unlocked her door and got inside as quickly as she could.

As soon as stepped over the threshold, she let out a little sigh of relief. The cool interior of the whitewashed walls welcomed her home. She didn't have much furniture. Everything she had served a purpose. With six children under the roof, some clutter was inevitable. But she did what she could to minimize it. Thankfully, the girls weren't home at the moment. Mrs. Ballas probably had them down at the market getting supplies for the week.

Constance glanced at Luca, watched as he walked around the open living room that led into her undersized kitchen. Her home must seem ridiculously small to him, but she loved it. Everything about it, from the deep, overstuffed sofa to the short bookcases lining the wall under the large windows was inviting and comfortable. Decorated in shades of blue, yellow, and white, her home was bright and cheerful and her heart soared with happiness every time she stepped through the doors.

The room seemed much smaller with Luca standing in it, but even he wasn't immune to its charms, it seemed. Some of the tension had loosened up his shoulders as he roamed around. She'd fully expected him to turn his pampered nose up at her humble home, but she didn't see any condescension in him when he turned back to her.

"It's charming," he said.

She laughed at his tone. "You sound surprised."

He shrugged. "Not sure what I expected. Some nightmare hive of filing cabinets and clipboards maybe."

She rolled her eyes at him and nodded toward several suitcases sitting by the door. The girls had been so excited at their upcoming "vacation" it had taken hours to get them to sleep. They'd each packed a bag, but she'd have to have Mrs. Ballas make sure they had what they needed. Constance hadn't been able to sleep at all the night before so she'd put her time to good use, packing everything she'd need for the long six weeks ahead.

"You can take those out to the car. I have to grab a few more things."

His eyebrows rose and she had to turn away so he wouldn't see her smile. She supposed it wasn't every day that the illustrious Luca Vasilakis played bellhop. It filled her with a surprising amount of pleasure to be the one to give him orders.

She went into her bedroom and grabbed her small overnight bag, dumping her jewelry box into it. Thankfully Mrs. Ballas had her own cottage next door or they'd have had to share the room. Constance wouldn't mind having the older woman live with her, but it did give them a bit more space without her there. And as Mrs. Ballas was technically a sort of housekeeper/nanny, having her own space gave her somewhere to hide when she needed a break.

Constance wouldn't mind hiding out for a while herself, but Luca was waiting. She went into the bathroom to gather her makeup and toiletries. She took a last look around, making sure she had everything. It wasn't like she couldn't come back if she forgot something. In fact, she was hoping to get away to her little refuge as often as she could. Surely she wouldn't have to spend twenty-four hours a day with Luca. She didn't think her sanity could stand it.

# Chapter Seven

Luca stepped into Constance's bedroom and looked around— bright, neat, and organized. Just like the rest of the house. Just like her. The bed with its colorful quilt was neatly made and while there were several soft pillows neatly arranged, it wasn't stacked high with decorative nonsense that never got used.

He pushed on the mattress a few times. A little soft for his tastes but definitely firm enough to support some vigorous recreation. He grinned, envisioning Constance's lovely face flushing bright red if he were to bring the suggestion up to her. He might just have to do that. Few things were more fun, he was discovering, than pushing Miss McMurty's numerous buttons.

A cushy looking chair next to the window sat beside yet another bookcase, a dresser with a mirror, and small end tables on either side of the bed. Everything about her home was comfortable and served a purpose, the complete opposite of his own home. Hell, he had entire rooms in his house he'd never even gone in. Bedrooms that had never been slept in. Knick-knacks he hadn't picked out. He'd always loved his house, but compared to Constance's place his house was more like a hotel than an actual home.

He flopped down on her bed and turned to the bathroom door. She came out and froze when she saw him lying there. Her eyes widened, her luscious mouth pursed with disapproval. He didn't bother trying to hide his smile. God, she was fun to tease. He lazily rubbed a hand over the spot next to him.

"Care to join me?"

Her lips pinched more. "No, thank you," she said, her voice cold and distant though her eyes roamed over his body and a blush stole across her cheeks.

"Come on. Why not give it a try and see how you like it?"

The pink in her face turned bright scarlet and she turned away from him, depositing a toiletry case and some bottles of shampoo and conditioner into a bag near the door. "You really are an ass, you know that?"

Luca barked out a laugh, surprised once again. "I've been told so once or twice."

She snorted. "I'm sure it's been more than once or twice."

He laughed again and swung his legs off the bed. She watched him come toward her, her eyes wary but unwavering. She didn't lack a backbone, that was for sure. Luca found it refreshing. He seemed to be surrounded by people only too willing to say and do whatever it was they thought would please him. She'd give it to him straight every time. He had the irresistible urge to needle her as much as he could just to see how she'd react.

She didn't budge an inch, even when he stepped so close to her only a breath of air separated them. Instead, she looked up at him, one eyebrow cocked.

"I can't quite figure out why you continue to feel it necessary to invade my personal space. Do you have a hard time hearing or seeing me from a respectable distance?

Maybe Joseph needs to make you an appointment for some glasses. Or a hearing aid."

He chuckled, the thrill of the chase running through him. He leaned closer until she was forced to take a step back. Right up against the wall. "I *like* being in your personal space."

She tried to frown but the expression didn't quite make it all the way. "Well, I don't like it."

"Now, that's not true." He placed one hand on the wall next to her head and lifted the other to draw a finger down her cheek. "Why do you blush every time I come near you then?"

"It's ninety degrees out and you keep insisting on forcing your body heat on me. It's not desire; it's heat stroke," she said, raising her pert little chin in the air.

His finger trailed down the column of her neck, skimming over the pulse beating furiously beneath her skin. He leaned in even closer, his lips hovering near her ear. "Why is your blood racing?"

"Because you're making me angry," she retorted, with a voice not quite as steady as it had been.

"Hmm." His fingers stroked along her collarbone and she shivered. What he wouldn't love to do to this woman. "I think you're lying…to me and yourself."

"I don't care what you think."

"That's not true, either."

She glared at him. "You don't know me, Mr. Vasilakis. So you're really not qualified to make that assumption, are you?"

He gazed into her eyes and could almost see her slapping her defenses in place. There was a sensual woman under the surface of all that control, begging to be released. He couldn't wait to see the passion she was capable of when she truly gave in to her own desires.

He closed his eyes briefly, trying to get a grip on himself. What the hell was he thinking? Yes, he wanted her, but she wasn't the type he could have fun with and then walk away from. He didn't know what it was about her, but he had a feeling she'd get under his skin, and that was the last thing he wanted. Too risky, too much to lose.

He glanced down, his eyes raking over her from her stylishly clad feet in their shiny new sandals, to her shapely legs, the hem of her white cotton sundress just skimming her knees, the dress merely hinting at the delicious body that hid beneath it. But most of all it was the intelligence and compassion radiating from those intense eyes that stared into his own, the strength and beauty that shone from her that she couldn't hide even if she wanted to. She was different, this woman, from any he'd known before. She was dangerous.

And still he wanted her.

He stepped away. He'd have to be content with the few tastes he got playing it up for the cameras. Anything else might lead down a road he had no desire to travel.

She watched him, her brow creased in confusion. He almost laughed. She wasn't the only one confused.

"Do you have all you need?" he asked.

She frowned, but nodded.

"Good, let's go. I'm sure Joe is anxiously waiting for us back home."

She nodded again and followed him to the door. Her bags were still sitting there but he gathered them up with a roll of his eyes.

"Can you get the door?" he asked, laying on the sugar-sweet sarcasm as thickly as possible.

"Of course." She grinned at him and opened the door.

The shouting began the second the door swung open. Constance gasped and jumped back, slamming the door shut again.

Luca sighed. He'd hoped to be able to ease her into the whole three-ring circus. Or at least run her through orientation. How to be a Stalked Celebrity 101. Oh well. A crash course would have to do.

"Walk straight to the car, don't look at them, don't hesitate, but don't duck your head. As long as they can get some shots, they might not press in too much. Do you have any sunglasses?"

She nodded, her face pale. "In my bag," she said, licking her lips. She fumbled around until she found them.

"Put them on. They'll help with the flashes. You ready?"

She nodded again, a little less sure this time, but ready to charge anyway. Impressive.

He handed her one of the bags so he'd have an arm free and took a deep breath. "Let's go."

He opened the door and ushered her out. The shouting came from all directions. People calling his name, asking questions. Who was she? Was it serious? Were those suitcases hers? Where were they going?

Constance kept her head held high and marched straight to the car, only pausing now and then when one of the men would crowd too close. Luca kept an arm around her, pulling her closer. Once again, he thought how stupid he'd been to head out without Joe. By himself, it might not have been so bad, but with Constance in tow there was a fresh story to be had. A juicy one. And everyone wanted to be the first to get a piece of it.

He plastered a smile on his face, tried to look good-naturedly bored, as if all the attention meant nothing to him. It did mean something, but the photographers probably wouldn't find it very flattering. So he did what he could to appease them. Besides, he and Constance needed to get in the papers; that was the whole point of their arrangement.

When they got to the car, Luca pulled Constance around for a second so the photographers could get some shots of them standing together.

"Smile," he muttered to her.

She glanced up at him, momentarily surprised, but she rallied quickly enough, letting a shy and overwhelmed smile show, though her face was still white as a sheet.

"All right, that's enough for now," Luca said, opening the door so she could slip inside.

The vultures moaned and kept shouting questions at him. Luca shoved the luggage in the trunk and headed to the driver's side.

"Sorry, guys. My fiancée is exhausted. I need to get her home. Thanks!" he said, sliding into the car amid a fresh wave of exclamations.

"What was that?" she asked him.

"What?" He eased out of her driveway, careful not to hit any of them. Not that it would bother him particularly if one of them got a teensy bit injured, but it would make his day more of a pain.

"I thought you hated them," she said.

"I do hate them. They hound me night and day no matter where I go or what I'm doing. The novelty of that kind of attention wore off a long time ago."

"Then what were you doing making us stand there and pose for them, and telling them flat out that I was your fiancée?"

"I thought you understood the whole point of this little charade."

"I do, but it seems strange that you'd court their attention when you say you hate it so much."

He shrugged. "They can be useful sometimes too. We need to get in the papers, on all the social media sites. Well, we just did. A couple good shots of us together here and from the store, that ring flashing on your hand, your luggage in the trunk of my car, and more shots of us pulling into my estate, and twenty minutes from now the whole world will know we're engaged. I'm sure the shots from the jewelry store are already being spread around with speculation as to what's going on. I confirmed it for them."

"I hardly think it'll be that fast."

Luca snorted. "Trust me. Face it, Miss McMurty. In less than an hour the whole world is going to know your face."

# Chapter Eight

Constance stared at Luca over a romantic candlelit dinner, trying to keep her face from revealing all the emotions seething inside. Anger being up front and center.

"I don't know why you're so upset. You agreed to all this."

"Yes," she said, smiling around her clenched teeth. "I did. Under duress. But you didn't tell me it would be like this."

"Like what?"

"Seriously?" she hissed, waving a hand toward the window of the restaurant where several dozen photographers had been snapping photos since the moment they'd sat down.

"You get used to it. Just ignore them."

"I don't see how anyone can get used to this."

He shrugged and took a bite of his spanakopita. "It can be a royal pain in the ass sometimes, I'll give you that, but I've found if you give them a good smile or two and then try to ignore them, they'll go away. Eat."

His tongue darted out to lick a flake of pastry off his lip and she froze with her fork halfway to her mouth.

Those moistened lips smiled and leaned closer to her. "If

you want a taste, all you have to do is ask."

Before she could register what he'd said, those lips made contact and sent little electric shocks rippling through her. It lasted only a moment and then he sat back down and resumed eating.

"We'll continue that later," he said, his eyes full of heat and promise. "Eat," he commanded again.

She rolled her eyes and tried to get a few bites down but it was disconcerting knowing people were watching them, and not just the ones with the cameras outside the windows. People in the restaurant stared as well. A few even snapped some pictures with their phones, not even bothering to try and hide what they were doing. Thank God the girls were home with Mrs. Ballas for the night. People taking pictures of them eating would have freaked them out, and he had to deal with it every time he left his house.

She sighed. "I'm sorry. I know I'm not making this any easier."

Luca put his fork down and sat back, his eyes blinking in utter surprise.

"What?" she asked. "Am I not being a pain?"

"Oh no, you're being a pain all right."

Her eyes narrowed and she tried to glare at him without everyone knowing she was glaring at him. Trying to convey what she was thinking and feeling without alerting the rest of the world to it all was exhausting.

"Yeah, I get it. I signed on to do this and now all I'm doing is complaining, but I really don't get it. Why are they so interested in me? I'm nobody." She glanced at Luca, confused but not sure how insulting it would be to ask for enlightenment.

"What?" he asked.

She waved him off but he frowned at her. "What? Just ask."

"I was wondering why you are so famous. Actors and professional athletes I can kind of understand. But you...well you sort of seem famous just for being famous. Like a Hilton or a Kardashian."

"All beautiful ladies who are surprisingly intelligent and genuinely nice people if anyone bothered to get to know them."

"Okaaay...but my point stands." She shrugged. "Never mind. I guess it doesn't matter. Seems odd to me, is all."

"It always seemed odd to me as well."

"Really?"

He took a drink of his wine. "Sure. I know people who have more money, who are better looking..."

She couldn't hide her incredulity fast enough at that remark and Luca rewarded her with a smile, the kind that had women throwing themselves at his feet. Great. That's all she needed to do, feed that already-over-inflated ego of his.

"Anyhow, I know people a lot more worthy of all the attention than me. So how did I get so lucky?"

"Really?" she asked, not believing a word he was saying. There was no way he was really that clueless.

"What?" he asked. He seemed genuinely confused.

"You don't think all your...escapades have had anything to do with keeping you in the papers? The cars, the houses, a different model on your arm every other week, the crazy parties even I've heard of? No offense, but your whole life seems to revolve around getting your name in the papers."

He wiped his mouth and set his napkin down on his plate. A little qualm of unease turned her already-rioting stomach. She hadn't meant to make him angry. He gestured to the waiter who hurried over with their check.

"I'm sorry. I didn't mean..."

He shook his head. "No. You're right." He cleared his throat and shoved his fingers through his slightly unruly hair.

He was impeccably dressed, as always. Tailored suit fitted to his perfect form so well she couldn't keep her eyes from roaming over him every few seconds. She'd taken care with her appearance as well, donning a dark blue dress she knew was particularly becoming, and a small blue butterfly necklace that matched her new ring, knowing that the cameras would be there, that people would be watching.

The sick realization that he had to do that every time he walked out of his house hit her. Who would choose that? To always be under that kind of scrutiny? She worried again for the children. It was bad enough she and Luca were hounded as they were, but they were at least adults who'd chosen the situation. The girls hadn't. She'd have to make double sure they weren't ambushed. No wonder Luca never wanted kids. Who'd want to subject their children to such treatment?

"You're right," he said again. "I do make it pretty easy for them. Habit, I guess. But then, they are there whether I make it easy for them or not. At least when I'm up to my antics, as you call them, I'm in control of the game. They see what I want them to see, most of the time."

Constance opened her mouth to respond. She hadn't thought it was possible but she was afraid she might have hurt his feelings. He didn't give her a chance to say anything else. He stood and held out his hand. She took it, let him help her rise. A server handed Luca a bag. He'd cleared their plates and boxed up the leftover food and she hadn't even noticed.

"*Efharistó*," he said, thanking the man and handing him a large tip.

She stole a glance at Luca, one eyebrow raised.

"You didn't eat much. I thought you might be hungry later."

"Oh. Thank you," she said, surprised. It was unexpectedly thoughtful.

He winked at her and raised her hand to his lips, keeping

his gaze locked on hers as he kissed her knuckle above her engagement ring. "It's my job to take care of you."

He sounded like he meant it. Again, she mentally chastised herself. She didn't know why she kept judging him so harshly. He really had been pretty decent to her, all things considered.

She gave him the sweetest smile she could muster and didn't object when he laced his fingers through hers. She'd deny it if ever asked, but she actually quite liked his big, warm hand enveloping hers. To her delight, he ushered her through the back door of the restaurant into a waiting car driven by Joseph. She settled back against the seat in the rear with Luca.

"Not that I'm complaining, but why didn't we have to wade through the sea of cameras out there again?"

Luca sighed. "Even I get tired of the circus occasionally, Stanzia. They've gotten enough pictures of us for the night. All I want to do is go home and get in bed."

Constance's stomach dropped to her toes. They were on their way back to his house, to his room, where she was expected to sleep in his bedroom.

They pulled through the gates of the estate. Only a few lights were on in the house. There was no party going on. No guests. No paparazzi (that she could see). No kids. It was the two them for the whole night, alone.

They entered the house and stood in the entryway. Luca turned to Joseph. "Make sure everything is locked up, and set the alarm."

"Of course, sir. *Kaliníhta*, Miss Constance."

"Good night, Joseph," she said, trying to keep her tone neutral.

Luca took her hand.

"Luca," she said, dragging her feet a little as he towed her down a hallway to a closed door.

"It's late. I'm tired. We're going to bed."

She tried to yank her hand from his. He held firm, but he

did glance over his shoulder, eyebrows raised in question.

"Something wrong?"

Protesting that she didn't want to go to bed would be both futile and a lie. She was exhausted. Nothing sounded better than curling up in bed and falling asleep. The problem was he'd be in the same room. Sometimes just being in the same town seemed too close to be to him. The thought of it made her body tremble and her mind race with fantasies that made her blush, and burn. If she survived the next few weeks, it would be a freaking miracle.

"No," she finally muttered.

"Good." The smug smile he gave her left her with no doubt he knew exactly what her issue was, and it amused him.

Well, that wouldn't do. She squared her shoulders, lifted her chin, and marched straight into his bedroom where she came to a complete, dead stop.

His master suite was almost bigger than her entire house. But the bed is what really drew her attention. She didn't know how big the dang thing was, but it was definitely larger than a king. Theoretically, this was a good thing. They could probably share it with no problem. In fact, if she lay near the edge on her side, and he lay near his, they could probably put another person between them, lying sideways. Plenty of space to avoid each other. Somehow, she didn't think it mattered how large the bed was. If Luca was in it, they would be too close. Thank God she was sleeping on the couch.

She realized he was watching her, his amused smile growing larger by the second. She tore her gaze from the bed and looked around for her things.

"Your luggage has been unpacked. Everything is in the closet here."

He led her to a closet that could have easily been a spare bedroom. One section of it now held her things. A small tinge of embarrassment settled over her at the thought of someone handling her things, especially her underthings.

"The bathroom is this way," he said, leading her to another large space.

The blue and yellow tiles of the bathroom reminded her of home. But that was as far as the similarities went. A massive tub, easily large enough for two, or four, filled one corner. A shower with more jets than she'd ever seen before filled another. It was large enough for a group and for everyone to have their own showerhead. The image of Luca standing under those steaming jets was a nice image indeed, but not one she should be dwelling on.

Her toiletry case had been set near one of the sinks and she went over to make sure everything had made it. Luca's steps coming up behind her echoed on the tiled floor but she didn't look up until his warm breath tickled her neck. Their eyes met in the mirror.

"Do you have everything you need?"

His gaze burned into hers and it took a second for her to gather her wits and nod.

"Good. You can have your turn in here first. I need to go over a few things with Joe anyway."

"Thank you," she said, her voice hardly more than a whisper.

He nodded but didn't move, just kept staring at her in the mirror. His eyes roamed over her figure and the look in them when they met hers again was enough to make her catch her breath.

He stepped closer, lightly wrapping his hands around her upper arms, keeping his gaze locked with hers until the last second. She held her breath, not sure what he was going to do. Not sure what she wanted him to do.

He pressed a chaste kiss to her cheek and then released her.

"I'll be back in a bit."

She nodded and watched him walk out the door, her heart hammering. As soon as he disappeared she slumped against the counter. Good gracious, that man would be her downfall.

She yelped when he stuck his head back in the door.

"By the way, I sleep on the left, in case you get cold and want to crawl in with me," he said with a huge grin, before disappearing again.

Despite the fact her nervous system was about to have a meltdown, an answering smile spread across her lips. His head appeared around the doorframe again.

"I also sleep in the nude."

Her mouth dropped open and he ducked back out, the bathroom ringing with his laughter.

# Chapter Nine

Luca wasn't sure whether to laugh or be offended. After Constance had nearly fainted from his declaration he'd be going to bed in nothing but the skin God had given him, she'd taken her pajamas into the bathroom, and then wouldn't come back out again until he'd turned out the lights, which he'd finally done in the interest of getting some sleep.

She headed straight for the couch, stopping short when she saw him stretched out on the overstuffed monstrosity.

"You can have the bed," he said.

"That's nice of you, but I'll be fine on the couch."

He shrugged. "But I'm already tucked in. Besides, you're my guest. You can have the bed."

She didn't say anything for a second or move to get into the bed and he sighed.

"Constance, just get in the bed. Let me be chivalrous for once. I assure you, it's not something that happens every day."

He heard a faint snort but she at least decided to take him up on his offer, darting out of the shadows of the room. She didn't exactly run to the bed, but she didn't take her time, either. He'd seen a brief flash of skin in the moonlight shining in from the window, but as she'd promptly pulled the covers up to her chin, he couldn't tell what she was wearing.

"I want you to know I find it highly inappropriate for you to be…you know…"

"Naked?" he asked.

"Yes."

He shrugged, not bothering to make sure the sheet stayed in place at his waist. "I doubt you'll believe me, but I'm not doing this for your benefit. It's more comfortable to sleep this way. Though I'm always hopeful I can entice you out of that frigid little shell of yours."

"I'm not frigid!"

"If you say so."

She huffed and he laughed. "We're engaged, Stanzia. There's nothing wrong with enjoying the company of your own fiancé."

"There's plenty wrong with it."

"Like what?"

"We barely know each other."

"So?" He pushed himself up so he was half sitting, half reclining against the arm of the couch. "We've got an amazing connection between us. I know you've felt it, so don't even try and deny it. If it's that good with just a little kiss, imagine how much better it could be."

The bright moon illuminated the room, showing her lying rigid in the bed, her arms crossed over her chest, the sheets tucked around her and pulled up to her chin. Oh, how he'd love to see her lose control. Be the reason she loses control. Just once.

"Our engagement isn't real."

"Says who? I asked, you said yes, I gave you a ring, we announced it to the world. How is that not real?"

"Seriously?" She sat up against the pillows to glare at

him. "You did not ask me to marry you; you blackmailed me into an engagement. You gave me a ring but without the intent behind it, it's just a piece of jewelry. And the same goes for the engagement. If we have no real intention of marrying, then it's not real."

"Well, regardless, I see no reason two mature, consenting adults can't take advantage of a sticky situation. No harm in it."

"There's a lot of harm in it."

"I don't see why."

She started to smile but bit her lip before it came to anything. "If you can't figure it out on your own, I'm not going to explain it to you."

Uh-huh. Classic woman response when they didn't really have an answer but were determined to win, or start, an argument.

"Well, you're going to have to put up with it. This is how I prefer to sleep and I'm not going to change it because there happens to be a beautiful woman in my bed. It would be more natural if you were to join me. It's almost criminal for you to cover that beautiful skin of yours."

He was only partially joking with her. His desire to see her naked, feel her skin against his, was so great his body throbbed with the need of her. She either felt the same way or was picking up on the vibes he was throwing out. Her eyes widened and he let the sheet drift lower over his hips. She scooted farther down beneath the covers.

"You keep scooting down like that and you're going to fall off the end of the bed. I'm not going to bite you, you know. Unless you want me to."

A quick intake of breath was hastily turned into a cough and Luca grinned into the darkness.

"Do you have to turn everything into a joke or sexual innuendo?" she asked.

"I don't *have* to, but it does make life a little more fun," he said with a laugh.

Her fight to keep a giggle in ended in a snort. She cleared her throat. "If you say so."

"I say so."

She finally gave in and chuckled. "Go to sleep, Luca."

She tucked the blankets more firmly about her and turned on her side away from him, huddled as far on the opposite side of the bed as she could get. Like that would stop him if he were really determined. Lucky for her, he had no interest in trying to seduce a woman who was clearly trying to talk herself into not wanting him…well, that wasn't really true. He had a lot of interest, but even he had some standards. He may have blackmailed her into a fake engagement, and he may enjoy teasing her now that she was in his bed, even if he wasn't in there with her, but he wasn't going to take advantage of her, unless she wanted him to. That didn't mean he couldn't have a little fun.

He wrapped his sheet around his waist and stood up. "Don't freak out. I'm just coming over for another pillow," he said.

One hit him in the face before he made it to the bed. He laughed and grasped the blankets, giving them a firm tug. She'd wrapped herself so tightly in them that she rolled toward him with a yelp.

"What do you think you're doing?" she said, slapping the blankets out of his hand.

"What are you wearing under there?"

"What?" she half gasped, half laughed.

"You jumped in bed so quickly I couldn't see what you're wearing. It's really something I should know."

"I can't see why," she said, trying to squirm back over to her side.

He was having none of that. He kept the blankets firmly

fisted in his hand. She was either going to have to stay put or leave the shelter of the covers.

"Because we are supposed to be engaged. We're supposedly sharing a bed. What if someone asks? It would be extremely embarrassing if I didn't know what my own fiancée wore to bed."

"No one is going to ask that!"

He shrugged. "You never know. I've been asked more intrusive things."

"Really?"

"You have no idea."

She stopped struggling, turning toward him with reluctant interest. "Like what?"

He eyed her suspiciously. "Why do you want to know?"

"I'm curious. Besides, you're my fiancé. Won't people expect me to know about your past?"

Throwing his own words back at him. Nice touch. He sat down and scooted up to lean back against the headboard. "People probably expect you already know. Everything I'm thinking of has already been in the papers. You'd be amazed at what reporters try to get answers to."

"I can imagine, and you just proved my point," she said with a triumphant smile. "If everyone else already knows then it can't hurt to tell me and it could hurt *not* to tell me, since I'll be the only one in the dark."

"Google interviews with me. I'm sure they'll pop up."

"Yeah, I'm kind of afraid of what else might pop up if I Google you."

Luca leaned closer. "Seeing as how you're lying in bed with me, I'd think you'd be more interested in what might pop—"

"Do *not* finish that sentence."

He chuckled. "You're no fun."

That strangled sounding, hastily cut off laughter escaped

from her again. "That's right. I'm not. So why don't you save me the trouble and tell me everything now?"

"I could, but then I'm not in the habit of giving away valuable information for nothing."

"I'd hardly call this information valuable."

He shrugged. "You're the one who wanted to know."

Her eyes narrowed as she tried to stare him down. She blinked first and a childish thrill of victory ran through him.

"Okay, what are your terms?" she finally asked.

Oh, he knew what he'd like to ask for. A modified version of strip Truth or Dare would be fun, but she'd never go for that. Maybe something similar but not quite as "daring" would fly?

"For every episode of inappropriate intrusiveness I tell you, you have to drop the blankets a few inches."

"What?" She gasped, but she exaggerated it. They both knew she wasn't all that surprised.

"I want to see what you're wearing, you want to hear my stories. Fair's fair."

One eyebrow rose. "Your obsession with my pajamas really isn't healthy."

"I'm aware of this. I still want to know."

She gave him a wry smile and shrugged. "If that's what you really want, deal."

"Oh, I didn't say that was what I really wanted, but I knew you'd say no to *that*, so I asked for what I thought I could get."

"And what do you really want?" she asked, leaning in just a hair.

His heart rate jumped a notch and all things south of the border perked up. He willed himself back under control. She was playing with him and every part of him seemed to understand that but his dick.

"Do you really want me to answer that?" he asked, his voice gone deep and husky.

Her breathing sped up and she shook her head. "I'm sure

I can guess."

"I'm sure you can, too, but since you refuse to go there, I guess we're stuck with the…safer arrangement. Agreed?"

She only hesitated a moment before nodding. "Agreed. So, tell me a story, and it better be good."

He laid back and put his hands behind his head. "Hmm, let's see. Okay, here's one. I once had a female reporter ask me how many times I could make a woman orgasm in one night."

"What? No way. What was the interview for? *Playgirl*?"

He snorted. "No. I would have expected questions like that in that case. I was doing a PR piece for the firm. My father had just purchased a large tract of land that had some significant historical finds on it."

Constance frowned. "What possible excuse could she have for asking you a question like that then?"

"I think she was asking for personal reasons."

That eyebrow of hers rose again. "I…I'm not even going to touch that. Okay, one point for you. Definitely an insanely inappropriate question."

"Good. Now, drop them."

Her eyes narrowed at him but the blankets dropped a few inches, baring her shoulders to the moonlight. Nothing covered them but a pair of thin, white camisole straps against her pale skin. He bit his lip, staring at the creamy expanse of her shoulders, at her collarbone, and the sexy little hollow at the base of her throat.

The longer he stared, the more she glared. "They're just shoulders. Everyone has them. They really aren't that interesting."

"So you say." He trailed a finger across the gentle slope of the one nearest him and she trembled under his touch, but she didn't move away. "You have exquisite shoulders, the kind that should be painted. Sculpted. Immortalized for all time.

Anyone who tells you they aren't worth staring at is lying. Or blind."

Her mouth dropped open a little but he wasn't going to give her the time to refute him. "I must see more. So another invasive moment. Hmm. Okay, I've got one. Actually, the question wasn't asked of me but asked of a friend of mine about me. Does that count?"

Her face puckered in that disapproving nanny way she had about her, but she nodded. "I'll allow it."

"A reporter once asked a girlfriend of mine how I measured up compared to other men she'd been with."

"No," she said with a little giggle.

"Yes. Thankfully, I surpassed the others with flying colors, so to speak. So, he offered her a hundred thousand dollars if she'd provide photographic evidence."

"Oh my God. She refused, of course."

Luca shook his head. "Nope. Sold me out less than twenty-four hours later. There I was thinking she wanted to spice things up a little and the next thing I know my penis is front-page news. Well, not front page…wouldn't want to scare the kiddies." He winked and laughed it off despite the fact that had been one of the most humiliating episodes of his life, not that he didn't think his favorite body part was spectacular, because it was, of course. But it had certainly taught him a valuable lesson in whom to trust.

"That's horrible," Constance said, the sympathy in her voice only making the uncomfortable knot in his gut tighten.

He tried to shrug it off. "Can't really blame her. It was a lot of money."

"Yes but—"

"I believe that's earned me more than a couple inches," he said, interrupting her. He didn't want sympathy from her. It was over and done with. He'd learned his lesson, moved on. He'd much rather focus his attention on the gorgeous woman currently in his bed, not some miserable ghost from his past.

He thought Constance might argue, but instead she lowered the blanket to her waist. He caught his breath and took her in. The thin silk of the camisole did nothing to hide the fullness of her breasts. If anything, the material accentuated the firm mounds that lay beneath it. Her nipples puckered, pressing against the thin fabric, and he had to twist his hands into the sheets to keep from reaching out to touch them.

The faint moonlight filtering in from the window made her pale skin glow like a freshly harvested pearl. The dark, wavy hair cascading over her shoulders just brushed her nipples and he ached to brush those tendrils aside and bring those tight little buds to his waiting lips.

"Luca?"

He blinked and brought his gaze back up to meet hers. She stared at him, somehow both amused and disapproving. "You seem surprised," she said.

He forced himself to get a grip. "I am, a little."

"Oh really? I know I'll probably regret asking this, but what did you think I slept in?"

"I don't know. Something flannel maybe. With sleeves down to your wrists and buttons up to here," he said, flicking a finger at her throat.

She slapped at his hand. "Oh, so because I have a houseful of kids and work with nuns I must dress like them, too?"

"Don't be so offended. You'd look amazing in a nun's habit."

She snorted. "Thanks. I think."

His eyes flicked over her again. "I could tell you what I hoped you slept in."

"Do I really want to know?"

He laughed. "Probably not."

"Too bad you won't be seeing the rest of it."

"Oh, I'm sure I can think of some more inappropriately

intrusive moments to get the rest of those blankets off."

She faked a yawn. "I don't know. I'm getting tired. It'd have to be a pretty good moment. Something *not* about your sex life would be great, if you even have any stories like that."

He knew one. It wasn't something he wanted to share, but the words were coming out of his mouth before he had made the conscious decision to speak.

. . .

"It's funny, I guess. I used to think all the attention was fun," he said quietly. "I'd purposely do the most outrageous things I could think of to get my pictures in the magazines. The paparazzi were almost like friends, there to immortalize me. Capture all my amazing moments. They made me famous for doing nothing, as you pointed out."

Constance bit her lip, wanting to apologize for her hasty words. Nothing she said ever seemed to faze him much. Maybe she'd been wrong. She held her breath, afraid if she spoke she'd spook him. She needed him to keep talking. The way he'd looked at her she was surprised her clothes hadn't melted right off. She was already having a hard time keeping her breathing slow and even, like she wasn't affected by the fact that she was lying in a bed with the sexiest man she'd ever seen, who, if she wasn't mistaken, wasn't wearing a stitch of anything beneath the sheet that covered him.

They weren't even touching, not even close. Aside from the brief brush of her shoulder, all he'd done was look at her, and she was ready to climb him like he was Mount Olympus… only he'd be the one planting his flag.

She closed her eyes, trying to shut out the sight of him long enough to get a grip on herself. And it was only the first night. How was she ever going to survive six weeks of nightly torture?

Luca took a deep breath and she glanced back at him. Some of her libido drained away at the look on his face. He was speaking, but not looking at her, just lying there staring at the ceiling, emotion raw on his face.

"The problem was," he continued, still staring at the ceiling instead of looking at her, "they didn't only capture the amazing moments. They captured *all* my moments. They once took pictures of me vomiting outside a club. That was attractive, let me tell you. I was too young to be there in the first place, too dumb to know any better." He laughed, but there was no humor in the sound.

"But the worst thing was the questions, always the questions. They'll ask anything, and I really do mean anything. Nothing is sacred to them if it'll sell a few papers. In fact, the more private, the better for them. You wanted to know what the worst, most invasive question I've ever been asked was?"

He glanced at her and it took all her will power not to flinch from the pain and anger in his face. She knew it wasn't directed at her but at some distant ghost of his past. Still, the sight made her want to curl up and hide, or maybe just cry for him. He didn't seem the type to cry for himself. She had wanted to know the answer to that question, but now she wasn't so sure she wanted to know what put that kind of pain in his eyes.

"The morning after my mother died, the paparazzi were waiting outside the hospital. When I came out they were screaming my name, taking their pictures as always. I tried to wave them off, asked them to give me some privacy." He laughed again and the sound almost broke Constance's heart. "You know what's stupid? I really thought they'd do it. I thought they'd back off. Not stick cameras in my face as I waited for them to wheel my mother's body out so we could take her to the funeral home. Not ask me how I felt over and over again. How did they think I felt?"

He shrugged and she reached over to lay a hand on his arm, hoping to offer some comfort.

"When they placed her body in the hearse, I broke down, sobbed like a baby right there on the street. Joe hugged me, kept his arms around me until we could get back inside. The moment he touched me, someone started asking if I was gay, if we were lovers. If my mother had known about us before she'd died and what she'd thought about it."

She squeezed his arm. "It bothered you they thought you were gay?"

"It bothered me they thought they had the right to ask about something so personal, something that was so beyond none of their business it truly amazed me they'd ask, especially in that moment, and that they'd connect it to my mother. My mother was being taken away so we could bury her and they are asking how she felt about my apparently fluid sexuality.

"Then one of them asked how much money I'd get. How much she'd left me. What was I going to do with my inheritance? Did we have life insurance on her that I'd get a piece of? Come on, you can tell us, how much did you get? Sorry about your mom, but at least you got something good out of it, eh?"

He swallowed hard and shook his head. "Did they think I cared about whether or not she'd left me anything? Or that any of that was any of their business? She was my mother. I'd have given everything I owned to bring her back."

"I'm so sorry, Luca. I lost my mother, too. I can't imagine…"

He nodded, breathing deeply for a moment before he spoke again. "After that I stopped trying to get their attention, but it didn't matter. They've never stopped following me around. And it doesn't matter what I do or who I do it with. So I do what I want, let them make up whatever they want. They'll do it anyway, no point fighting it."

Constance had no idea what to say to any of that. Her throat tightened with unshed tears at the young man he'd been, and for the disillusioned man he'd become. He didn't seem the type to welcome sympathy, and there was precious little she could do to erase years of pain. "I'm so sorry, Luca."

He shrugged. "Doesn't matter now."

"Of course it does."

He looked at her, though she wasn't sure he really saw her. "It's in the past. It's how life is."

Constance squeezed his arm but he shook his head. She let go, wishing desperately she could take some of the hurt from him. Yes, he was an egotistical, often manipulative control freak, but he'd just proved even he had feelings. Even if there was nothing she could do to make things better for him.

But she could at least try and take his mind off it a little.

"Well," she said, "you certainly kept up your end of the bargain. So here you go." She whipped off the blanket so nothing covered her and was rewarded by the haunted look fading from his eyes as he took her in.

Had she'd known the morning before that she'd be spending six weeks in a gorgeous billionaire's bedroom, she'd have purchased more appropriate pajamas. Well, more conservative was probably a better word. At home, alone, she liked to sleep in little scraps of silk that were cool and soft against her skin. She didn't own anything other than sets of camis and shorts like the one she was currently wearing, except for the silk nightgowns that she thought might be even worse in her current situation.

She knew the pajama set did nothing to hide her curves from his hungry, roving eyes. She'd worry about that later. For the moment, she was just happy to see that it had chased the shadows from his face.

"Satisfied?" she asked.

The laugh he gave this time was deep and male and held no hint of sorrow. "Oh, Miss McMurty, not even close."

She smiled. "That's too bad, Mr. Vasilakis. Now go back to your sofa and go to sleep."

"You aren't going to give your fiancé a kiss good night?"

"Nope."

"Oh, so cruel, Stanzia."

"Good *night*, Luca," she said, mortified when a giggle escaped before she could rein it in.

She yanked the covers back over her and turned on her side, comforted by his quiet laughter in the darkness.

# Chapter Ten

Luca stood in his front doorway, unease rolling through him. He'd faced down hordes of reporters, ex-girlfriends with serious revenge issues, and once an entire rugby team he'd taunted mercilessly through their defeat. He'd been more comfortable in all of those situations than he was at that moment.

The van he'd been watching pull into his driveway came to a stop. Before the motor had even shut off, five little girls jumped out and rushed toward him. He stood back to let them pass, although his instincts screamed at him to bar the door. No good could come of this.

Constance alighted from the vehicle, following behind the first rush much more slowly, her hand held firmly by a sixth little girl, the one who'd been pulling up his flowers. His eyes narrowed. To his surprise, she glowered right back at him. He was kind of impressed. She was a tenacious little thing. She just better stay away from his flowerbeds.

They were followed by the sweetly plump Mrs. Ballas who patted the handkerchief tied around her graying hair before ambling to a stop beside Constance. She glanced back and forth between Luca and Constance, her cheeks growing redder by the moment.

"Mr. Vasilakis, you remember Mrs. Ballas from the Family Aid organization?"

"But of course," he said, kissing her hand. "Welcome to my home."

She giggled and batted him away before hurrying inside after the children.

"And this is Elena," Constance said, nodding down at the little girl holding her hand. "You met the other day."

"So we did," he said, staring down at her. She was a beautiful child, really, if she'd get that scowl off her face. "You were the one ripping up my flowers."

She stuck her chin in the air, but kept silent.

"Don't touch anything," he ordered.

Elena stuck her tongue out at him and let go of Constance's hand, running inside to join the others who, by the sounds of it, were already destroying his home.

Constance folded her arms and frowned up at him.

"What?" he asked.

"She's a child, Luca, for heaven's sake. You don't need to be so…gruff."

He smiled at that and pulled her resisting form into his arms. "I was laying down the ground rules. Children need rules."

"Oh, they do? And how do you know anything about children?"

She kept her arms folded across her chest like a shield, but she didn't struggle against him.

"I know enough." He leaned down and brushed his lips across hers. To his delight, she responded, her mouth moving under his. But when he would have deepened the kiss, she pulled away.

"Luca," she murmured. "The children might be watching."

"So?"

She blew out an exasperated sigh. "I don't think it's appropriate for us to be…intimate in front of them."

His eyebrows rose at that. "I agree. If we are going to be intimate, I want you alone so you can scream my name as loud as you want."

Her mouth dropped open, her cheeks flaming red. Luca laughed and she pushed away from him.

"You are so…uncouth," she said, trying to walk past him.

He caught her hand. "That I am. Never pretended to be otherwise."

A half smile tugged at her lips. "Well, that's true enough."

"I was simply stating my opinion that a rather chaste kiss is appropriate enough for the kids to handle."

"Chaste?"

"This, on the other hand, probably wouldn't be."

He pulled her back into his arms, his mouth descending before she could break free. The moment his lips touched hers, she stopped trying. Instead, she sank into him with a sigh of pleasure that had him angling his head so he could delve deeper. She tasted of lemon and honey and Luca couldn't get enough.

His hand trailed down her waist and she broke away with a little gasp. She stepped back, a bit shaky, and reached up to pat her hair back into place.

"We shouldn't," she said, not meeting his gaze. "The girls might be watching."

"More importantly, other people might be watching."

The frown was back and he hated to be the one to chase her smile away, nor did he want her to think that the watching vultures were the only reason he'd kissed her. They hadn't even entered his mind until she'd pulled away. He'd just wanted to kiss her. He'd spent most of their moments together wanting to kiss her, among other things. After spending a sleepless night lying on that damn sofa, listening to her softly snoring in the dark, his entire body begged for some attention.

But it didn't hurt to remind both of them what they were really doing there. His revelations the night before had put a new softness in her eyes when she looked at him, and a new tenderness in his heart when he looked at her. He'd never told anyone what he'd told her last night. There was something about her that made him want to open up, spill his soul, and that should be the last thing he wanted to do with a woman, especially an attractive one half naked in his bed. They both needed to remember this was a business arrangement. There was no room for heartfelt confessions of any kind.

"Let's go inside then," she murmured, stepping into the house.

He brought her hand to his lips for a gentle kiss. Her eyes widened but she smiled and the knot in his gut loosened a bit.

He followed her into the house where absolute chaos reigned. Mrs. Ballas stood next to his housekeeper, who watched the scene before her with one hand over her bosom, the other over her mouth. The maid who had come in for the day to help set up the children's bedrooms watched in total amazement as six little girls turned his couches into trampolines while screeching at the tops of their lungs.

"Quiet!" Luca shouted.

Seven pairs of eyes stared at him in astonishment, including Constance's.

"Sit," he said, jabbing his finger at the couches.

The girls dropped onto the sofas and watched him warily.

"Mrs. Lasko has made some snacks for you, and some movies are being set up for you to watch. You will eat and watch the movies with minimal noise and mess. Is that understood?"

The girls all nodded. Constance watched him, biting her

lip like she was trying to keep from laughing.

"What?" he asked her.

"You want the girls to sit quietly through several movies? Without making any mess at all?"

"I fail to see why that's amusing."

She cleared her throat but the amused smile remained. "Which movies did you get?"

He had no idea. He glanced at Mrs. Lasko who proudly said, "*Barney*."

Constance grimaced which sparked a frown in Luca. "What's wrong with *Barney*?"

Constance's eyebrow rose. "Nothing. They don't get to watch many movies, so I'm sure it will be fine."

"But?"

"But…Barney is a large purple dinosaur generally more popular with younger children."

His frown deepened. "They don't look all that old."

"The songs also have an annoying tendency to get stuck in your head for days at a time. It drives me nuts. You, I think, will be absolutely certifiable by the end of the day."

"You underestimate my mental acuity."

She shrugged and smiled at him. "We'll see."

He ignored that. "Mrs. Lasko, is their food ready?"

She nodded and quickly exited, dragging the maid behind her.

"Mr. Vasilakis—" Constance started.

He interrupted her, irritated by her sudden formality since the arrival of the children. "Stanzia, my ring is on your finger. You spent last night in my bed. Call me Luca."

Her mouth opened and closed a couple times, her face red as the merlot they'd had for dinner the night before. Her eyes darted around the room at their audience. Luckily, only the girls remained and they were too busy using Joe as a May pole to have heard what he said. Her priority was, of course, making sure the girls didn't know about their sleeping arrangements and continuing the whole vacation-with-a-friend story. He, on the other hand, needed the world to think their engagement was real. Their charade would never work if she wouldn't call him by his Christian name. Maybe they could spin it as a nickname, calling each other Mr. and Mrs. Vasilakis.

That thought made his stomach drop, though he wasn't entirely sure if it was a bad feeling or not. It was odd.

Constance recovered herself and tried again.

"I addressed you so for the children's benefit, but if you prefer it, fine. *Luca*. Even if I could get them to sit through one movie, multiple movies will bore them to tears. Even if it was something they wanted to watch. If they are going to be in your home then they need to be able to do something that will actually keep them entertained."

"Such as?" he asked. The thought of the little heathens running wild through his house was going to make him break out into hives. Yet another reminder, as if he needed one, of how incompatible children were with his life.

"The only thing here for them to do is swim, so let them use the pool. They brought their suits."

Luca folded his arms across his chest. "Isn't that how this whole thing started? Letting them use the pool now would be like rewarding their bad behavior from last time. Besides," he said before she could protest, "Nico is still trying to get the pH balance of the pool right after they were in it last time. I don't know what they threw in there but I nearly had to drain the thing and start from scratch."

"It wouldn't be like that this time. They know how to behave. They're just bored. They're children, not dogs. You can't tell them to sit and stay and expect them to wait for your next command."

Luca frowned at her. He knew she had a point but he

didn't want to acknowledge it.

"Fine. I will make sure Joe either has something more suitable for them to do or we will take them somewhere or something. I'll send him out right now for a truckload of toys. But for right now, can they sit and watch the movie? I don't think it's going to kill them."

She sighed. "Fine. However, while we are on the subject…"

He groaned and rubbed a hand over his face. "What now?"

"If the children are going to be in your home, there are a few things I'd prefer you didn't leave lying around."

"Such as?" he asked, his irritation rising again.

"Just off the top of my head, you've got a bar in the corner where the liquor is out in the open. Your entertainment center is stocked with movies that are highly inappropriate for children…and a few that are highly inappropriate for adults as well."

He grinned at that one, but let her continue without comment.

"You have cigars and matches lying about. Your coffee table is made of glass and has sharp corners. If one of the girls were to trip, it could be disastrous. They aren't toddlers, of course, so I don't think we need to childproof the entire house, but kids do tend to get a little rambunctious now and then so I figure it's better to be safe than sorry. There are—"

Luca held up a hand to stop her. His head was already pounding and they'd been there only five minutes.

"Enough, Stanzia. Give it a rest." He pulled her aside, out of earshot of the girls. "This is my house. I'm not changing anything because a bunch of kids happen to be here for a few weeks. If they are too old for Barney, I'm sure they are old enough to know to keep their hands off booze and matches. If not, remove the dangerous items yourself but leave the rest alone."

She opened her mouth to speak again, but he didn't let her get that far.

"If you'll excuse me for a minute, I need to take care of a few things in my office."

Her eyes narrowed for a moment. Then her face cleared and she gave him a sweet smile that he didn't trust for a minute.

"You go right ahead and do whatever you need to do."

He smiled at her. Finally. "Thank you. Joe," he said, gesturing for the man to follow him.

Constance nodded at him and he said, "*Kalimera*, Miss McMurty," bestowing a brilliant smile on her as he extracted himself from the girls and made his way to the office.

"*Kalimera*, Joseph. And please, call me Constance."

"As you wish, ma'am. Sir," he said, turning his attention to Luca. "I have the items you asked for. I've placed them on your desk."

"Thanks, Joe."

"I'll go join the girls," Constance said.

Luca nodded absentmindedly. "I'll be in my office for a bit."

"Don't mind us," Constance called over her shoulder.

# Chapter Eleven

Luca watched her leave, admiring the way her hips swayed back and forth when she walked. The cutoff jean shorts she wore complimented her figure far more than those hideous khaki things he'd first seen her in, and he'd thankfully broken her of those hideous sandals.

When she disappeared into the kitchen, Luca turned to find Joe waiting patiently for him with an amused smile that he tried to hide by turning quickly away. Luca chose to ignore it. Calling attention to the fact that he'd been ogling her would only make matters worse.

Joe followed him into the office and closed the door.

"Do you have those papers from the office I need to sign?" Luca asked him.

Joe nodded and pulled out a briefcase. Luca went through his paperwork as fast as he could, wanting to get that out of the way before some wayward child came crashing through his office door. His father had been surprised when he'd jumped back into the work pool and shown a renewed interest soon after their meeting, but he hadn't hesitated to include him on the new projects they had in the works. Luca had forgotten how much he enjoyed working with his dad, being involved in new real estate ventures, scoping out locations and developing new properties. He just needed to find a way to balance it with some sort of social life so he didn't become a total workaholic like his old man.

Once he had all the relevant contracts signed for the new project his father had assigned to him, he turned back to the other papers on his desk.

"How's our plan going?" he asked Joe.

"I've pulled up the main sites and there are a selection of the usual papers on your desk. All carry the pictures from the jewelry store, of course. There's lots of buzz online about the ring, several flattering pictures. There are a few, however, that Miss McMurty might find objectionable."

Luca snorted while browsing the different websites. "What *doesn't* she find objectionable?"

Joe didn't answer that but instead pointed out the article in question on his computer screen. Someone had been doing their homework. While most sites offered up the usual information on Constance, this one had gone a bit deeper. They'd reported she was the daughter of James McMurty, whom she had said worked at the embassy. He was the United States ambassador to Greece, something she'd neglected to mention, but the journalists had discovered quickly enough. They detailed her schooling, her rather boring yet educationally impressive resume, and her relatively new situation as a House Mother, but it didn't stop there.

The world wanted to know who Constance McMurty was, and they weren't being scrupulous about finding out. Her whole life story was written in those pages, things Luca had never dreamed were a part of her past—like her abandonment at an orphanage when she was three. Her adoption by the ambassador and his wife two years later. The death of her adoptive mother a few years after that. He never would have guessed she'd suffered so much.

He flipped through a few more sites. They all had pretty much the same images and info. There were a few pictures that he hadn't expected, however, and Constance probably wouldn't be happy.

A loud crash and the sound of someone running past his door jerked his attention away from the computer.

"What the hell was that?"

"The sound of six children in your house, sir," Joe said.

"I was aware of that much," Luca said, giving him the sarcastic look that remark deserved and headed for the door.

He marched down the hallway to the great room. The site that met him had him frozen in shock.

The girls scurried everywhere, their arms full of his belongings. Constance sat on the couch in the center of the room, supervising the depositing of those belongings into boxes, while Mrs. Lasko and the maid stood by watching, their faces etched with wary amusement, until they caught sight of him. Then all amusement fled and only the wariness remained. Smart women. They were right to be worried.

Constance, on the other hand, looked up at him with a smile, seemingly oblivious to the fact that she was allowing the children to ransack his house.

"What the fu—"

"Sir," Joe said, shaking his head.

Luca glared at him but minded his language. After all, he wouldn't want to corrupt the little kleptomaniacs who were looting his house.

"Constance, what in the ever-loving hell is going on?" he asked, keeping his voice just under a shout by sheer force of will.

She blinked at him innocently. "You said if I wanted to remove the dangerous items in the house to go ahead. So I am."

He snagged an R-rated movie out of the arms of a passing kid who looked like she'd just robbed a Redbox and held it up. "How is this dangerous?"

"Aside from the rating, it's a horrible movie. Totally inappropriate for children."

"And you think they might accidentally pop an R-rated movie into the Blu-ray one night and have a go at it, do you?"

She shrugged. "You never know. Better safe than sorry."

He was really starting to hate that phrase. He stared at her, so dazed with astonishment he wasn't sure how to react. Another kid hurried by with a bottle of Ouzo in each hand.

"Hey, you…"

"Lexi," Elena supplied helpfully.

Constance looked up in surprise but Luca was too busy chasing down the Ouzo thief to notice much.

"Give those back," he said, making a grab for them.

She made it to Constance and the box she was amassing before he caught up with her.

He stood in front of her, fists clenched at his sides as he surveyed the damage. His shelves had been stripped bare of anything even slightly objectionable, his bar had been cleaned out, and even the coffee table had disappeared.

Constance stood and looked him straight in the eye. His anger faded a hair. Pissed or not, he couldn't help but be impressed that she could hold her ground when he was less than six inches from her and ready to seriously spank someone. The sudden image of the prim and proper Miss McMurty squirming over his knee in carnal delight was a delicious thought…

"Girls, why don't you take a break for a minute? Go make sure your belongings are put away neatly in your rooms."

She waited until they'd scurried off before turning back to him. "Look, I know you're angry," Constance said, pulling him out of his daydream and back to the nightmare of reality, "but you told me I could get rid of the dangerous stuff. I was doing what you said."

"Oh, don't give me that innocent act. That would be like me telling you to kill a spider and you burning my house down around my ears."

"It's not that bad," she said with a little pout.

"Not that bad? Not that bad? Are you serious? I meant you could put away the matches, maybe even lock the liquor up in the cabinet. I did not give you permission to clear out my house."

"I'm sorry, Luca, but I cannot allow the children around these things. You had an antique fishing spear above your mantel for heaven's sake!"

"The children should be well enough behaved to stay out of other people's belongings."

"They are well behaved, usually."

"Then there shouldn't be an issue with a spear on the wall as a decoration, or a few R-rated movies on my shelves. Or liquor in the liquor cabinet where it belongs."

Constance stared him down. There was quite a bit more he'd like to say to her but he'd wait to see if she'd crack first.

"All right, I'll put some of it back."

He opened his mouth to argue but she cut him off.

"I'll concede most of it, as long as you put the movies on a high shelf or something and keep the liquor locked up, and promise not to drink around the children."

"You can't be serious."

"I'm very serious. I'm responsible for these children. I won't have them subjected to a drunken…" She gestured at him, unable or unwilling to finish her sentence.

"A drunken what?" he asked, his anger fading into amusement. The woman had balls, he'd give her that.

She huffed. "You know what I mean."

"Yes, I'm afraid I do. Not a very flattering image you have of me."

"I don't mean any offense by it," she said.

"Too bad. Offense taken." No way was he letting her out of this that easy.

But she surprised him again.

"Fine, be offended, as long as you abide by my wishes." She folded her arms across her chest, putting her metaphorical foot down.

Two could play at that game. "This is my house. You'll abide by *my* wishes."

"You're the one who wanted the children as part of the arrangement."

"That's not true. I just wanted you."

She blinked up at him, her lovely mouth open with an inaudible gasp.

"The kids were Joe's idea," he added.

They both turned to look at him.

"It's going lovely, too, if I do say so," Joseph said with a pleased smile. "Nothing but good press today."

Luca's eyes narrowed. The man was diabolical. Brilliant. Indispensable. But diabolical.

"As I was saying," Constance continued. "If you want the children to be part of this, you've got to be willing to make some concessions."

"Your *concessions* are turning my life upside down."

Her lips twitched upward. "Yes, children have a way of doing that."

Reminding him yet again why he never wanted any. They'd been in his life only a few hours and he didn't even recognize his own home anymore. Granted, if he had his own children they'd hopefully arrive one at a time. Maybe they were easier to handle if you started out slow. Then again, the sight of the box Constance had going, full of his favorite things that were apparently not kid-friendly, was a nice visual of what he'd have to give up for the privilege of signing away his life.

"You're enjoying this," he said. "In fact, I think you're just doing it to torture me."

"That wasn't my intention, but I'll admit, it's a nice fringe benefit."

He tried to glare at her but he couldn't maintain the expression while she gazed up at him with that flirty, mischievous twinkle in her eyes.

She stepped closer and put her hand on his arm.

He looked down at her in surprise.

"I'm not asking for much here, Luca. Don't drink or smoke around the children. Keep the dangerous substances under lock and key just in case. And the coffee table stays gone. That thing is a million stitches just waiting to happen."

"All right. I'll concede. But…" he said, stopping her before she could let her triumph show too much. "You'll have to concede something as well."

"What?" she asked, her voice full of suspicion. She had a right to be suspicious because what he wanted she wouldn't want to give up.

"I'll tell you that a bit later. When we have less of an audience," he said, nodding at the children who had filed back into the room and stood watching the two of them.

Her eyes narrowed, but finally she nodded. "Fine. Later then. But for now?" she said, nodding towards the girls.

Luca sighed. "Fine. Go swimming."

The girls jumped and screamed and then ran for the bedrooms, he assumed to put on their suits. All except Elena. She just looked at him.

"What?" he asked.

Constance frowned at him but Elena tilted her head. "Thanks for the pool."

"You're welcome."

"I'll stay out of the deep end."

"That would be a good idea."

"And I won't touch the flowers."

Luca resisted the urge to smile. He got the impression the little girl in front of him would take that the wrong way. Instead he responded as seriously as she had. "Thank you."

Elena nodded. "You're welcome." Then she turned without another word and wandered off to find the other girls and Luca turned back to Constance, who stared at him like he'd suddenly announced he was becoming a priest.

"What?" he asked again. He was starting to sound like a parrot, echoing everything he said.

Constance shook her head, bemused. "I don't think I've ever heard Elena thank anyone for anything before. She's a quiet child." She tilted her head to peruse him, much as Elena had. "She must like you."

He snorted. "Don't sound so surprised. It has been known to happen on occasion."

A faint blush staining her cheeks. "That's not what I meant."

"I know. I guess me and the kid understand each other, that's all."

Her brow furrowed like she was trying to figure it out, then her face cleared and she gave him a grateful smile.

"You know what? I'm not even going to question it. I'll be thankful and move on."

"Really? Are you feeling okay?" he said.

She gave him a mock glare and turned to follow the girls out to the patio.

Luca grabbed her hand again before she could leave.

"They're fine where they're at. Mrs. Lasko and Mrs. Ballas should be back there with them." He looked at Joe for confirmation. He nodded and Luca continued. "We can go out in a minute, but we need to see how things are going first."

She frowned. "What do you mean?"

"I'm assuming you haven't been online yet this morning? Or seen the papers?"

Her frown deepened. "No. I assumed there would be pictures of us, as that is the whole point of all this. Are there not?"

"Yes, but they've surpassed even my expectations."

"Why don't you sound happy about that?"

Luca glanced at Joe who nodded and left them alone. Luca led Constance into his office and sat her down at his desk. He already had several of the worst media sites pulled up so she could see the photos.

"I'm not unhappy necessarily, but I don't think you'll be happy about how intrusive they are being. I thought you should see."

Constance didn't say another word but scrolled through the sites. Pictures of them at dinner, walking through town, in the jewelry store, pictures of them kissing. She finally paused on the one he knew would upset her the most. Someone with a long-range lens had managed to get a shot of them in her bedroom. Luca, with his arm braced against the wall, leaning toward her. Constance, her upturned face looking like she was waiting for his kiss.

"They took pictures of us *inside* my home?" she asked, her voice faint. "I knew they'd take pictures everywhere else, but…can they do that? I mean legally? We were inside my private property."

"Legal doesn't mean much to them if it will get them a juicy picture."

Constance took a deep breath and blew it out. Then she stood, pushing away the papers laid out for her before she'd gotten through the whole stack.

"I'm not going to lie and say I'm happy about all this,

but I did sign up for it. I knew it would happen, to an extent anyway. If you can put up with it every day of your life, I can manage for a few weeks."

Luca stared at her, shocked into silence for probably the first time in his life. He'd expected her to…well, he wasn't sure. Cry, maybe. Get angry, certainly. But this calm acceptance? Never.

She hadn't seen what they'd written about her past. His Constance had been through a lot in her life. Enough that he could understand the rigid control she tried to keep over everything.

It was that desire for control that made her acceptance of her current situation all the more incredible. She seemed to be taking it all in stride. He should probably tell her about the other article, though she probably already at least suspected they'd have dug around in her past. Still…

She smiled at him and reached up to pat his cheek, like she knew the confusion that was currently running through his head.

"I never much believed in crying over spilt milk, as they say. It's done. I can't change it. And to a certain extent this was our purpose to begin with, so we can hardly fault them for doing what we want them to be doing. After our discussion last night…" She glanced up at him, barely meeting his eyes before looking away again. "Like I said, this is your life. You'll have to deal with it forever. I can make do for a few weeks."

Her mention of the night before brought back a few delectable images he would have loved to dwell on but she didn't give him the chance.

She rose up on her toes and gave him a quick kiss on the cheek, shocking him for the second time. "Now, let's ignore the vultures as best we can and go see what the children are getting into."

"Oh God," Luca groaned. He wasn't sure he wanted to

know.

He was right. The girls were splashing about in the pool like they were under attack from a shiver of sharks, and were screaming just as loudly as if they were. He wasn't sure how there was enough water left in the pool to actually swim in— most of it seemed to be on the patio. The women watching them had apparently given up trying to keep any sort of order. Mrs. Ballas sat on a lounge chair watching the chaos with a bemused expression on her face.

Elena was the only child not going completely crazy. She hung on the edge of the pool in the shallow end, staring out to sea. He couldn't really blame her—it was an incredible view. With his house perched on a cliff, swimmers in the pool got an unobstructed view of the crystal clear turquoise waters of the sea. If he wanted to get closer, a path ran down the rocky hill to his own little slice of sandy shoreline, but from the pool, you could see for miles. The coastline of the island, crammed with whitewashed buildings with their bright blue and red roofs, the sailboats coming in and out of the harbors, the larger ocean liners and yachts farther out.

The little girl had found one of his favorite spots to just sit and contemplate, but he was a thirty-year-old man who'd gone through enough in his life to be jaded and cynical and in need of some natural therapy. She was a little girl, five at most. What sorts of things could be running through her head to keep her from playing like her friends in their newfound paradise?

"What's with her?" he asked, nodding at Elena.

Constance bristled. "There's nothing 'with' her." She went back into the house, beckoning him to follow.

His interest piqued, he followed.

Constance glanced back outside before she spoke. "The other girls are all foster children, but Elena is an orphan. Her parents were killed in a car accident last year. She has no other relatives and needed a home. I'd already taken on more than I planned with my five girls, but she and Magdalena were friends and we thought she should be with someone she was close to. So I took her in. She's a good girl, but she doesn't talk much. She loses her temper frequently. I try to be there for her as much as I can, but she doesn't really let anyone get close."

Luca watched the little girl, not joining in on the fun even when the other girls tried to include her.

"You're worried about her," he said.

Every time she looked at Elena, Constance's whole being shifted, like she was trying to pour positive energy into the little girl just by sheer will, not unlike what she had done with him the night before.

"Yes," she answered. "She seems to like being in my company, but she's been through too much and I can't take it away, though I wish with every ounce of me I could. There's only so much I can do for her."

She gave him a half-hearted smile and went back out to sit beside Elena.

Luca frowned. The sadness he'd seen in her eyes created an ache in his heart he didn't know how to deal with. What was this woman doing to him? He'd known her two days and already he was willing to rearrange his life just to put a smile on her face. Had she been anyone else that might not have been such a problem, but this particular woman would turn his life upside down and bring a whole lot of noisy, destructive baggage along with her.

Still, he wanted to try, and the thought shook him to his core.

"Joe," he said.

The man was by his side in a second. "Yes, sir?"

"I know we can't keep the photographers controlled all the time. But no more inviting them along; they have enough pictures of us."

"Arrangements have already been made for a few sessions with you and Miss Constance. I'm afraid if we cancel those, they will try to get shots in a less civilized manner."

Luca sighed. "Fine. We'll honor whatever arrangements have already been made, but no new photo ops. And I don't want them anywhere near the children. I want extra security measures taken when they are with us. It's one thing for them to get pictures of me, but the kids don't need to be involved. No more leaks about me spending time with them. No more mention of them. They are here for a vacation. That is all."

"Sir…"

"Is that understood?"

Joe nodded. "Yes, sir."

"Good."

He turned back toward the chaos in his backyard; toward the little girl at the edge of the pool in particular. And the woman sitting beside her. There might not be much he could to ease the pain of their pasts. But he could help ensure he didn't instigate any in their futures.

It wasn't enough. But it was a start.

# Chapter Twelve

Constance held her breath, her heart twisting with the emotions rushing through her. Luca had been busy with work for the last week and as a reward for closing his first solo deal since returning full time to the firm, he'd surprised them all with a day of horseback riding on the beach. Organizing six children with enough adults for each child to ride with was the definition of chaos, but things had gone relatively smoothly.

Constance was already mounted and Magdalena sat in front of her. Mrs. Ballas had shocked Constance by springing onto the back of her small mare like she'd been doing it her whole life. She took Lexi up with her. Each of the other girls rode with staff from the riding company except Elena. Elena had watched quietly while everyone got situated and then walked over to Luca, raising her arms up to him.

He glanced at Constance with something like panic but had bent to lift the child onto the horse, swinging up behind her. He rode over to her side, his brows lifting when he reached her, his eyes looking from Elena, to Constance, and back again. She just shrugged with a smile she knew was both pleased and amused. She didn't know what it was about Luca that appealed to the little girl…maybe she sensed the same sadness in him that she carried with her. Maybe it was as simple as the fact that Luca was about the only man in her life. Whatever it was, she'd taken a shine to Luca, which seemed to disconcert him to no end. Constance would be lying if she said she didn't find that at least a little amusing.

"Quit smiling," he playfully growled at her, which only made her smile bigger.

He smiled back and she had half a second for her suspicion to spike before he reached across the space between them and grabbed the back of her neck, pulling her to him for a quick but thorough kiss.

Magdalena giggled and he let go, winked at Constance, and spurred his horse into a trot through the surf.

Constance glanced around, blushing at the indulgent and amused smiles of the adults, the giggles of the girls, and the outright anger on the face of one of the guides. She stared at her, for a moment not sure what she'd done to earn the woman's scowl, then she realized the other woman must be jealous. A spark of pride and possession burned in her chest. Temporary or not, Luca was hers and whether it was all an act or not, he made no secret of the fact that he wanted her and enjoyed her company. Any other women could just keep their jealousy to themselves.

She nudged her horse to a trot, following the path Luca had taken through the surf. He smiled at her when she caught up and her heart filled with joy at the expression on Elena's face. Luca earned so many brownie points because of that bit of happiness, she didn't protest once at his repeated stolen kisses and slightly inappropriate behavior throughout the afternoon. By the time they'd returned the horses and finished the picnic dinner they'd packed and the girls were drowsily roasting marshmallows in the fire Luca and the men had built,

Constance was ready to concede just about anything to him. It had been an amazing day, thanks in large part to him.

So when he slid down behind her next to the fire, wrapping his arms around her and pulling her back against his chest, she didn't hesitate to snuggle into him. They watched the sun sink into the sea while he nuzzled against her neck, murmuring nonsense in her ear. She didn't even care if it was for real or for show. The few photographers that had tried to get near the group had been chased off by Luca's security. A surprise, to be sure, since she thought he wanted "proof" more than anything. But a welcome one. She cuddled closer to Luca and pretended it was all real.

Once the sun had set, Joseph and Mrs. Ballas loaded the girls into the van he had waiting to take them back to the house. Joseph would stay behind with another guard as inconspicuous security while Constance and Luca had their own private photo op. A necessary evil to keep the circus at bay when possible. She wasn't sure what he had in mind. He'd earned a lot of goodwill and cooperation from her that day, but she wasn't going to have sex on the beach or anything, no matter how wonderful Luca had been.

Luca left her for a moment to have a quick word with Joseph, who stood with the other guard a discreet distance away. Close enough to help if they needed it, but far enough away they had at least the illusion of privacy. Luca came back with a guitar in one hand and a bottle of champagne and two glasses in the other.

She raised an eyebrow. "You play?"

"Occasionally," he said, his lips stretching into a slow, sexy smile that had her heart pounding and her body aching for him.

If he could do all that with a smile, she was a goner if he touched her.

He set the guitar down and opened the champagne,

handing her a glass. She sipped a little too quickly, needing something to take the edge off. With the girls gone, things had gone from safe to intensely intimate, even with the lurking presence of security and the paparazzi she figured were out there somewhere.

It didn't help that he wasn't speaking, just sitting there, drinking his champagne and watching her watch him, that smile still on his lips, sitting so close the heat from his body warmed hers even though he didn't touch her. He knew the effect he was having on her. Damn him. He was enjoying every second of it.

"It was a wonderful day, Luca. Thank you," she said when she couldn't stand the silence anymore.

"You're welcome. I found it rather pleasant myself."

"You sound surprised."

"I am. I've always loved to ride. Having you in front of me while we rode would have been immensely pleasurable. We'll have to do that next time."

The heated promise of those words had her breasts tightening and warmth pooling low in her belly. She took another hasty sip of champagne, ignoring his quiet, smug chuckle.

"Anyway," he continued. "I didn't expect to enjoy today as much as I did, with all of our additional company. It was a bit surprising."

"I'm glad you had fun," she said.

He picked up the guitar and absently strummed a few chords, tuning the strings and plucking out a few notes. The firelight flickered over him, highlighting his chiseled features, the biceps that bunched as he played. His fingers moved across the strings and she shivered, too easily picturing those fingers moving over her skin. She had no doubt he'd play her just as well.

The few notes he'd been picking out solidified into a song,

one of her favorite songs. He played very well. She found herself smiling as she swayed to the tune, her eyes closed. When he started quietly singing, her eyes flew open and she sucked in a small breath of surprise. His voice floated to her, deep and smooth. Her gaze met his and held, those dark eyes burning into hers while he sang.

*Ach koritsi mou.* Oh, my girl.

She breathed in one shaky breath after another as he sang about the unrevealed parts of his soul belonging to her. How he'd waited so long for her to come into his life, and every time he sang the words *ach koritsi mou* it was like he was laying claim to her, branding her as his.

His voice died away with the last note of the song. Still they sat staring into each other's eyes. He put the guitar down and her breathing sped up as he leaned in. She watched him until their lips met, then she closed her eyes and gave herself over to him. She wrapped her arms around his neck, her fingers tangling in his hair. He hauled her closer, pressing her down into the sand. His lips left hers to trail down her neck and she arched against him, trying to bring him closer.

"*Koritsi mou,*" he murmured against her skin.

My girl. Oh yes, she was his. It might not last. It might not be real in the harsh light of day, but for that moment, on the sand beneath the soft moonlight, with the salty breeze of the sea flowing over them as he moved over her, kissing her until her body begged for more, she was his, totally and completely his.

He broke away, pulling back so he could look into her eyes. Whatever he saw there must have pleased him. He brushed her hair from her face, his smile somehow both tender and possessive. His hand stroked down her side, his thumb brushing across her breast. She trembled beneath him, wanting more, needing more. He leaned down to recapture her lips and her eyes fluttered closed again.

Someone cleared his throat and Constance gasped, her hand flying up to cover her face. The whole "I can't see you, so you can't see me" theory had never actually worked out, but it did help to close out the sight of Joseph's uncomfortable face.

She couldn't believe she'd forgotten they weren't alone. Had he forgotten? Or had he been aware, maybe even counting on the fact that someone out in the bushes was taking pictures to sell to the highest bidder? She knew she had no right to be angry. He hadn't tricked her; she'd known they had an audience. Apparently, the key to making her completely forget everything was a sexy Greek god singing to her in the moonlight.

"Sorry," he said, taking her hand to pull her up. He kept his arm around her waist, drawing her close for another kiss. She was angry but…she sighed, melting against him. Who was she kidding? She had no defense against him.

He reluctantly released her. "Got a little carried away there," he said with a slight laugh.

That assuaged her embarrassment a bit. At least he didn't seem to have purposely started a make out session for the benefit of the cameras. She hoped.

He leaned in close to whisper in her ear. "Why don't we take this back to house where we won't be interrupted?"

Her heart thudded. She knew what he was saying. If they picked up where they left off, somewhere where they were alone, with a bed, it was going to go all the way. Hell, if Joseph hadn't interrupted them, they might be well past the point of no return right there on the beach.

Luca watched her, waiting for her answer. She wanted to so badly she literally ached, but if she gave in now she was just setting herself up for heartbreak when the whole charade was over. She'd never been a casual sex–type person, and she was already starting to care for him more than he'd ever care about her. Sleeping with him was a really bad idea.

She opened her mouth to tell him no. "Yes," she whispered.

The look of sheer carnal promise Luca aimed at her sent a fine tremble running through her. He drew her in for one last kiss and then took her hand to lead her to their waiting car.

She couldn't believe she'd said yes. She should take it back. Tell him she'd changed her mind. But as she settled against him in the backseat of the car, his arm pulling her close, his hand tangling in her hair while he trailed kisses over her heated skin, she knew no matter how badly she might regret it in the future, she wanted this, wanted him, desperately.

She'd deal with the future later.

• • •

Luca couldn't believe she'd said yes. He expected her to shoot him down immediately, but she hadn't. His body thrummed, impatient, greedy. He wanted all of her right then.

When they arrived at home, the house was quiet, the kids and Mrs. Ballas tucked up asleep in their wing of the house. Luca barely paused to nod good night to Joe before marching to his bedroom, his hand entwined with Constance's. He pulled her into the room behind him, kicked the door shut, and had her up against the wall, his body holding her captive.

Her eyes widened, their deep blue centers dark with desire. Her mouth dropped open, her breaths coming in little pants. He throbbed, ached. He pressed against her, growing even harder when her eyes fluttered and a little moan escaped her lips.

He leaned in close. "Is it still a yes?" he asked. He'd die if she said no, but he wanted to make sure she knew what she was getting into and was on board one hundred percent.

She opened her eyes, staring into his for a moment before smiling, then she trailed her hands up his chest, pushing his shirt up so she could skim over his nipples until they pebbled under her fingers. He yanked his shirt off over his head, giving her better access. On the way back down she applied her nails, pressing hard enough to draw a growl from him. She leaned forward, pausing with her lips a breath away from his.

"Yes," she said. "Please, yes."

That was all he needed to hear. He closed the distance, his mouth devouring hers until she whimpered and moaned. He bent to lift her. She wrapped her legs around his waist, crying out when the hard length of him pressed against her center. God, her wet heat radiated through their clothes. They needed to come off. Now.

He turned, marching across the room to the bed. He let her slowly slide down the length of his body, biting his lip as every inch of her rubbed against him. His hands moved under her shirt, lifting as he went. She raised her arms and he slipped her shirt off over her head so he could push her bra aside. His hand closed over a breast and she moaned, arching into him. If she kept doing that, he'd never last.

He left her for a second to grab a condom out of the drawer of the nightstand.

"I'm on the pill," she said. "And all was well at my last physical."

"Same here. Minus the pill part," he said with a grin.

"Guess it doesn't hurt to double up."

His smile grew wider. He rolled the condom on and nudged a leg between hers, his heart hammering. He lowered himself, an arm braced on either side of her head, letting her feel his weight without crushing her. Her breath hitched. The sound sent his pulse thundering in his ears. She wrapped a leg around his waist and he bent his head to reclaim those lips.

A scream ripped through the night and Luca jerked up. He knew the sound hadn't come from Constance but looked her over anxiously just in case. She was already pushing off the bed, grabbing her shirt and whipping it back over her head.

"Elena," she said, running for the door.

Luca's heart pounded again, for an entirely different reason. *What was wrong?*

He ripped the condom off, yanked on some sweatpants, and followed Constance at a dead run through the house. Mrs. Ballas met them in the great room, holding the little girl in her arms.

Elena let out another wail and Constance reached for her. She quieted down, her screams reduced to great hiccupping sobs.

"I've got her, Mrs. Ballas, thank you."

The woman nodded, glanced briefly, eyes wide as sea urchins at Luca's shirtless chest, and then turned to leave them.

Constance was crooning softly to Elena, swaying on her feet. He glanced at her, not sure what he could do to help. She motioned to the sofa and he nodded, following her as she sat with Elena on her lap.

"She has nightmares," Constance quietly explained.

He sat beside them and looked down at the little girl again, his heart twisting. Poor little thing. He reached out a tentative hand, looking to Constance for permission. She nodded, a bit hesitantly. Maybe she wasn't sure how the child would react. He took it slow, gently stroking Elena's hair back. She didn't protest, just looked up at him with large, dark eyes, her thumb in her mouth.

He continued to stroke her hair as she blinked sleepily against Constance's shoulder. Memories of his mother doing the same thing for him flooded his mind, and he began to hum. The same tune his mother had sung to him whenever he'd been sad or afraid.

Constance glanced up, surprised, but a gentle smile

touched her lips. He wrapped an arm around her shoulders and leaned down to kiss her forehead, keeping up his rhythm stroking of Elena's hair. And then he began to sing low and soft over and over, while Constance slowly rocked.

Luca wasn't sure what time it was when Elena finally released a deep, tremulous sigh and drifted off into sleep. All he knew was that his heart ached for the little girl, and the rest of him wanted to sleep.

He helped Constance up and walked with her to the room Elena shared with Lexi and Irene. She carefully laid the little girl back in bed and tiptoed out the door.

"Will she be okay?" Luca whispered. They stood at the door and watched a moment, but Elena seemed to have settled into a deep, contented sleep.

"I think she'll sleep now."

She headed back toward their room with him in tow, climbed onto the bed with a choked sigh and gathered a pillow to her chest.

"Hey," he said, settling down beside her. "What's wrong?"

She didn't answer for a moment but her eyes grew shiny. Finally she shook her head. "I don't know what to do for her. When her parents were killed in the car accident last year, she was with them—the only one to survive. She still dreams of it. There was no one else who could take her in. She lost everything, her parents, her home, everything. No child should have to go through that. I just wish…I wish I could take all that pain from her. I feel so helpless…"

The tears slipped down her cheeks unnoticed by her, though each one seared his heart like drops of acid.

"*Shh*, don't cry. Come here," he said, pulling her onto his lap. "It's all right, Stanzia, I've got you."

He held her and rocked her while sobs wracked her body. He knew exactly how she felt. He'd have given anything in that moment to take away her pain, to make it all better. The best he could do was hold her while she cried, stroke her hair from her face, and murmur soothing nonsense into her ear.

After a while, the sobs grew softer and then stopped altogether, her body lay limp and heavy in his arms. He sighed, resting his cheek on her hair. She'd cried herself to sleep. That was definitely a first for him. When they'd started the night he certainly hadn't expected it to end up like this.

He settled her gently against her pillow, climbing in beside her before pulling the sheets up to cover them. She wiggled back against him and then fell back to sleep with a sigh. Luca's body instantly reacted and he released a sigh of his own.

Well, it might not have been how he'd pictured their evening going, but there were worse ways to spend a night. He wrapped his arm tighter around her and closed his eyes, breathing in her sweet scent as he drifted off to sleep.

# Chapter Thirteen

Constance stood at the water's edge, letting the sea lap against her toes while she watched the girls play in the surf. She closed her eyes for a second, lifting her face to the sun. This was why she'd fallen in love with Greece. The thought that some ancient woman might have stood in the same spot she was, the same breeze blowing through her hair, the same sea spread out in a glistening turquoise field before her. The beauty and history of the place renewed her, energized her. She could breathe for the first time in over a week.

Spending her days traipsing around town with Luca and nights caring for Elena while trying to convince herself she didn't want to be in his bed had taken their toll. Even to herself she couldn't pretend there wasn't an attraction there. The man was sex on a stick and she was having a hard time resisting him. The moment may have passed but after their near miss a few nights before, her resistance was becoming more and more futile. She'd only been able to hold out since then because opportunity had been scarce. She might be able to think a little more clearly when she wasn't nearly naked in his arms, but that hardly mattered anymore. The fire had been lit and it was consuming them both.

The reason for the scarce opportunities had resolved itself, which meant her brief reprieve was over. Elena was finally sleeping on her own, without insisting Constance stay with her all night. Whatever had triggered her nightmares seemed to have passed, for the moment, which meant Luca would be expecting Constance back in his room. Maybe even back in his bed. She didn't even try to lie to herself again about whether or not she wanted to be there. She wanted it with every fiber of her being. It was her sensible mind that was causing the headache.

A shadow joined hers in the waves moments before strong arms slipped around her waist. She tensed for a moment, and then let herself lean back into him with a sigh. There were some advantages to a legally binding job to act like a loving fiancée. A tough job to be sure, but someone had to do it, and it allowed her to relax and act as she wished without the constant barrage of *what ifs* and *should I's* running through her head.

Luca nuzzled at her neck, his lips leaving a trail of fire everywhere they touched.

"You look so beautiful standing here in the sun," he said, his arms tightening around her waist.

"You don't have to say things like that, you know. They can't hear you from wherever they are hiding."

"Wherever who is hiding?"

"The vultures you invited."

He pressed another kiss to her neck. "I didn't invite any photographers today. And those that managed to find us anyway are hopefully being kept at bay by my security. I'm not saying anything for anyone's benefit. I'm saying it because it's true."

Her stomach did a little flip and she fought the urge to

sigh like a schoolgirl. The man was smooth, she'd give him that.

"What do you mean, no photographers? I thought that was the whole point."

"Not anymore. They've gotten their story. They'll get what pictures they can when we're in public. We don't need to invite them into private moments."

"Yes, but…"

"Forget them." He lightly grasped her chin, turning her face to the side so he could look into her eyes. "I mean it, Stanzia. You're like my own Aphrodite rising from the sea. You take my breath away."

He brushed a thumb down her cheek and she shivered against him.

"You're very good, you know that?"

He smiled. "Yes, I do. And if you weren't so stubborn, you'd know it too."

He kept her face turned toward him, his thumb moving up to stroke her bottom lip.

"Luca, the children might be watching."

"I don't care."

He stopped any further protests with his lips, his mouth moving over hers until she forgot where they were. Nothing existed but the man whose arms held her, whose lips were wreaking havoc with her good intentions, whose hand had crept from her waist to move up her rib cage toward the breast that ached for his touch.

*Wait…*

"Luca," she said, spinning out of his arms. "Behave yourself."

She reached up to pat at her hair, her eyes darting from the children who were having lunch on the sand and completely ignoring them to the security team keeping the few tenacious paparazzi who had hunted them down cornered behind a wall of well-muscled men. At least they wouldn't be able to snap a hundred pictures of Luca trying to cop a feel.

"Sorry. I can't seem to keep myself under control when I'm around you."

He didn't look the least bit sorry. In fact, he looked pleased with himself, in need of a lesson in humility. Constance backed up slowly, going deeper into the sea. Luca followed, as she'd known he would, stalking her like a shark would its prey. She waited until she got about shin deep and then kicked at the water, sending a huge spray raining down on Luca. He shouted, looking at her in shock while water dripped from every chiseled muscle.

"Oh, now you're in trouble."

He lunged for her and she shrieked, laughing and tripping in the water trying to get away. She didn't get far. Two strides and he was on her, picking her up and running deeper into the water with her.

"Don't you dare!" she yelled.

He laughed, wrapped her tighter in his arms, and jumped backward, dragging them both beneath the waves. Constance came up sputtering.

"I can't believe you did that!"

He shrugged, but the happy, carefree grin on his face warmed her to her very soul. That was his real smile, the one he never showed the world. Seeing it made her dousing well worth it. Of course, that didn't mean she wasn't up for a little revenge, but before she could do anything, he'd grabbed her around the waist and hoisted her up. Her legs bicycled in the air, but she was laughing too hard to disengage herself.

He put her down, turning her to face him. Before she had time to second guess him or protest, his lips were on hers. His hands tangled in her hair, keeping her imprisoned. Not that she had any complaints. She wrapped her arms around his neck, standing on her tiptoes so she could press herself closer.

The movement of the waves knocked her off balance, but Luca held her tight, his mouth plundering hers and making her head spin even as his body kept her anchored.

She was about to climb him like a Corinthian column so she could wrap her legs around him when the hoots and shouts from down the beach finally penetrated the sex-crazed haze that fogged her brain whenever he touched her.

Luca put her down, his smile gone. He glowered in the direction of the photographers. Constance had actually forgotten for the moment they were there. She laid a hand on Luca's face and turned him back to face her.

"Looks like a few got through security. Play nice for the cameras," she said.

"They'll be dealt with."

She wasn't sure if he meant the photographers or the security who'd let them through. And who'd thankfully regained control. Probably both.

He gazed down at her, his frown turning into a smile that sent fire zipping through her.

He hauled her back to him and gave her a swift but thorough kiss.

"I'd rather be alone with you so we could continue what you started."

She looked up at him. "What I started? You started it. I just got you a little wet, that's all."

He closed his eyes like she'd hit him in the gut and lowered his forehead to rest on hers. "Yes, you did, and I'd seriously love to repay the favor, only I won't get you a little wet. You'll be soaking through those proper panties of yours."

She pulled back with a gasp, though she wasn't so much outraged as turned on like she'd never been before. How did the man make her body beg for him with only a few words? Her mouth opened, but instead of berating him, she leaned closer.

"Mama Stanzia!" a little voice called.

Constance jerked back. The girls were done with lunch… and had probably seen way too much. Luca had a way of making her forget everything and everyone but him. She pulled away from him but he held onto her for as long as possible, those dark eyes of his staring down into hers.

"I better go play with the children for a bit," she said. They called her over again and she waved. The girls had called her Mama Constance before but had taken to using Luca's nickname for her. She still wasn't sure how she felt about that. She loved it. Her heart lurched every time she heard it, but it would be a painful reminder when their time was up and they went their separate ways.

His gaze flickered up to the girls scampering on the beach. "I'll join you in a bit. I better…take a swim first."

She followed his gaze down to where the evidence of how much he'd enjoyed their game jutted through his swim trunks just below the water. Her mouth dried. She couldn't tear her eyes from him.

"Stanzia," he said quietly, his voice thick with amusement.

"*Hmm*?"

"While I would love to finish what we started, I'd rather not do it with quite so many witnesses."

Constance jerked back into awareness and hastily stepped away, her face burning.

"I…I better go," she stammered.

He caught her hand and brought it to his lips. "Later," he said.

Before she could respond, he turned and dove beneath the waves, surfacing a few feet away. His strong arms pulled him through the water, farther away from her. She watched him for a moment, swimming in one direction. Her girls waited for her on the beach, in the opposite direction. A nice little visual of the conflict going on in her head.

Luca. Or her girls. She couldn't have both.

Luca had made it clear how he felt about kids. He might play nice while he was forced to, but he'd said he never wanted kids, and she had six of them.

The girls were her highest priority. They needed her. Even if Luca were open to having the kids as a permanent part of his life, there was no place for them in his world. What kind of life would it be having paparazzi stalk their every move? Invading their privacy, snapping pictures of their most vulnerable moments the way they'd done to Luca. Even his security couldn't keep them safe all the time. She'd seen what that kind of upbringing had done to him. She couldn't allow that to happen to her girls, even if Luca wanted them all, which he didn't. The girls had had enough people abandoning them. So had Constance.

Luca...he was amazing, larger than life. A dream. And like a dream, he wouldn't last. Even if he thought he wanted to be with her, accept her and the kids, it wouldn't last. Their lives were too different. He'd get tired of the restraints that having six kids would place on his life. He'd move on like he always did. She'd seen the headlines. It was never him getting dumped. He was always the one moving on to someone else. It would be painful enough when he walked away from her when their agreed upon time was up. But if she allowed them to get closer, to continue this relationship, maybe make it real...when it crashed and burned he wouldn't just be leaving her. He'd be leaving the girls as well. Constance wouldn't let it happen again to them.

She had a little time, time to live in the fantasy, but that's all this was, a fantasy, and it would be over soon. And when it was, they'd all go back to their real lives. The girls would have pleasant memories of their vacation with Constance's friend and she...well, it would hurt less than if she tried to stay and make it work only to watch it crumble.

There really was nothing to think about. There was no choice to be made. She took a deep breath, gathered what wits she could, and went to join the girls on the beach.

. . .

Luca swam until his arms trembled. Constance was going to be the death of him. She filled his every waking thought, and most of his sleeping thoughts as well. He'd never forgotten where he was or who was watching before, and yet there'd he'd been, standing in the sea about to make love to her with a bunch of kids, his security team, and several uninvited photographers watching.

He turned and began a slow swim back, enough energy burned that his dick had given him a break and stood down, for the moment anyway. All it would take was one look from Constance and it would be right back, ready for action. He didn't think she even realized the effect she had on him, or that she looked at him like he was a sticky sweet piece of baklava she couldn't wait to sink her teeth into. A few more of those looks and he'd have her up against the wall, no matter who was watching.

He made it back to the shore, thrilled to see that Joe and his security had finally gotten rid of the photographers. Luca wasn't naïve enough to think they were all gone, but the group on the beach had disappeared at least. He scanned the shore until he located Constance walking along the beach with several of the girls, gathering seashells. A couple more played in the sand, but Elena sat off on her own. Interesting child, though he could understand the desire to be alone.

He hesitated before going over to her. He really had no business being anywhere near any child, let alone one with the issues that Elena had. The last thing in the world she needed was someone like Luca in her life, no matter how briefly. Trying to befriend her might do more harm than good, couldn't it? He mentally snorted. Who was he kidding? Being associated with him did most people more harm than good. Which was one of the main reasons he'd decided he'd never have kids. Aside from the whole fact that he liked his freedom and kids were the fastest way to destroy that, Luca didn't want the responsibility of being in charge of anyone else's life. He'd screwed his own up enough.

He looked at little Elena, thought about how it would feel to be responsible for her happiness and well-being. The thought filled him with a terror so strong it actually made him take a step back. She'd been through enough without subjecting her to his messed up world.

Still, he hated to see her sitting there all by herself. It seemed so…lonely. Lonely was something he knew a little bit about, too. He walked over to where she sat and stared down at her. She barely paused in her sand castle building to glance up at him, but she didn't protest him being there so he sat down beside her. She handed him a stick and kept on with her digging and building. He held it for a second and then shrugged. All right then.

They worked in silence for a good half hour. She'd scurry off every now and then to bring back buckets of water or seashells to decorate their masterpiece. To his surprise, they not only worked very well together, but he enjoyed it. Maybe he needed a hobby. Sitting in the sand, sculpting it into some semblance of a castle, was cathartic in a way. Calming. A nice escape from his life. Best yet was when Elena looked up at him when they were finished and smiled. The sweet expression pulled at heartstrings he didn't know he had. Then she climbed onto his lap and he froze. She curled up with a little sigh.

"Hey now, what are you doing?" he asked. He couldn't just shove her off his lap. But he wasn't remotely comfortable with her being there. He'd never held a child before. Not even a baby. Well, except after Elena had fallen in the pool.

She shivered and he automatically reached for the towel that lay just behind them and covered her with it. She cuddled into his chest and closed her eyes. Within minutes she was asleep. Luca looked around, helpless.

"Luca, look over here!" someone called.

He turned toward the voice, already shielding Elena from the camera he knew was snapping away. He would have yelled at the jackass, but he didn't want to wake the child. Luckily, Joe hovered nearby as always.

"Get them out of here, Joe," he said.

"But sir, isn't this what we wanted? It's a great photo opportunity. Shows your softer side."

Anger flashed through Luca strong enough that Joe blanched and stepped back. He was irritated a lot, but seldom truly angry, and Joe knew the difference.

"This isn't a photo op, Joe. I told you. No pictures of the children. Get him out of here. *Now*."

"Yes, sir," Joe said, turning to mobilize security.

Luca scooted around as best he could without jostling Elena. If there were any more lurking photographers, all they'd get were pictures of his back.

He looked up to see Constance watching him, a soft smile on her lips. She came and settled down beside him, leaning over to kiss his cheek. Such tenderness filled his heart to the point he had to look away. What was going on? This was all supposed to be a sham. Sure, he'd hoped he could talk her into his bed for real, but these…emotions weren't supposed to be part of the deal. Emotions made things complicated. He didn't do complicated.

"Here," he said, passing Elena over to Constance before she could protest.

"She likes you," she said, nodding down at the sleeping

child.

He snorted. "I don't know why."

"Oh come on, give yourself some credit. You aren't that bad," she said, her mouth twitching up.

"What a rousing stamp of approval."

She ducked her head. "I meant it as a compliment."

"You might want to work on those."

Her smile grew bigger. "You aren't as bad as I'd feared, let's put it that way. Still, you could be better."

His eyebrow rose. "Oh really? Better how?"

She shrugged. "Spend less of your time partying, more time doing some good in the world. With great power comes great responsibility."

Both eyebrows rose at that one. "Did you just quote Spiderman to me?"

Constance ducked her head again with an embarrassed little chuckle. "Maybe, but the premise stands. You have all this power that you could be doing so much good with, but you do nothing with it."

"I don't have power, I have money. There's a huge difference."

She shrugged. "Not really. With money you have the power to change things, make people's lives better."

"So, I should give all my family's money to charity."

"No, of course not, but instead of buying another car you won't drive or more clothes you won't wear, you could be putting some of it toward something worthwhile. You wouldn't even miss it, yet it could change someone else's life."

Luca frowned, but he couldn't really argue with her. There were six cars in his garage at the house on a small island where it was easier to walk or ride a motorcycle than drive. And he had more at the other houses he owned in other countries. Someone could easily sell half of what he owned and he probably wouldn't even notice.

"I wasn't talking about your money though," she continued.

He frowned. "Then what were you talking about?"

She nodded at the retreating photographers still fighting to get through security on the other side of the beach. "You say you have no power, but you do."

"The vultures?"

She gave him a faint smile. "You say you hate them, but you're willing to use them when it suits your purpose. You use them to change people's opinions, to manipulate the way they think."

Luca's frown deepened. He didn't like her assessment, but again, she wasn't wrong.

"You wanted to be seen differently. So you found a fake fiancée and a bunch of children and let the vultures loose, and already the tide's turned. The party boy has become the responsible family man, someone people would be comfortable with running their company. Like it or not, what you do matters to people. What you do influences their decisions and actions. So how would it be if the party boy turned family man becomes the philanthropist, championing those in need?"

Luca stared at her, not sure how to respond. She was right. Not a fun thought to admit to, but there it was, and it had been something he'd been feeling for a long time—a desire to have more to show for his life. To have something associated with his name that his mother would have been proud of, something worthwhile.

"You have power, Luca. More than perhaps you know. You have the power to lead by your example. What you need to decide is which example do you want people to follow?"

Her eyes searched his with an intensity that made him want to squirm. He stood and brushed the sand off his ass. "If you'll excuse me, I need to speak with Joe for a minute."

She looked like she was going to say something but he didn't give her the chance. He needed to get out of there before he did something really ridiculous like pledge his fortune to charity and vow to become a monk.

Joe fell into line with him the moment he walked by.

"Joe, no more photo ops. Cancel the rest of the sessions we had scheduled."

"Sir?" Joe asked, his eyes wide.

Luca almost snorted. All the things this man had seen him do and he'd never batted an eye, but *this* shocked him.

"I'm done. I don't want the photographers around anymore. They've gotten enough pictures. Call them off."

"Yes, sir," he said, still frowning. "Will Miss McMurty be leaving then?"

"No," Luca said, too quickly. A slight twitch of Joe's eyebrow indicated he'd caught the panic in that word. Shit.

"No," he said, more calmly. "We'll keep up the engagement story for now. But we don't need an audience anymore."

Joe nodded. "Yes, sir."

Luca nodded and turned back to look at where Constance sat, gently rocking Elena. His heart jumped again and he turned his gaze out to the sea for a moment before addressing Joe again.

"Make sure Constance and the kids get back safely. I have a few things I need to take care of."

"But sir…"

"I'll take security with me."

"Yes, sir," Joe said, his brow furrowed.

Luca didn't bother to explain himself. He had too many thoughts and long-forgotten emotions running through him. He needed a little space to sort them all out. Hopefully when he came back, he'd have everything under control again.

Because God help him if he didn't.

# Chapter Fourteen

Several hours later and Luca still didn't have his shit pulled together. Coming home only made it worse.

Walking in the door, he tripped over a Barbie doll but kept his swearing to an internal monologue in case any of the children were running around. There were signs of them everywhere. Sweaters and shoes and toys and crayon drawings. He didn't even know where it all came from, although it seemed Joe always had a new toy in his hand when he'd come back from wherever he disappeared to during his off hours. And yes, Luca may have been guilty of that, too.

Still, he hadn't thought they'd accumulated so much. Signs of himself in the house had dwindled. The spear from over the mantel had been removed to storage along with the bottles of liquor that Constance had confiscated the first day and anything else that could remotely do any harm to the kids.

Coming home to a house changed by the eight females currently in his life didn't bother him. But shouldn't it have? He should have been irritated that his space had been invaded, that they had come in and changed everything. But he wasn't.

If anything, it was comforting to come home and know the house was full and he wasn't alone.

He tried to shake off whatever was going on with him. He just needed some sleep. He'd wandered the island for hours, riding his motorcycle as fast as the streets and trails would allow. He'd ignored every attempt his so-called friends had made in drawing him back into the party life, with relatively little effort. In fact, it was surprising how little he missed that scene. The slow seduction going on was killing him but the growing closeness with Constance had made him happier than anything else in his life ever had. A realization that terrified him more than he'd like to admit.

Now there he stood, looking down at her while she slept. Having her back in his bed sent a thrill through him that was only partially due to the possibilities it presented. The fact that she was curled around his pillow sent a happy little spark straight to his heart. That she slept in the tiny cami and shorts ensemble sent a stronger spark a little farther south. He couldn't go on with her in his bed night after night while he slept on the sofa, never being able to touch her. Especially after what had happened the last time they were alone in this room. He'd go mad.

Luca went to the closet and stripped down, this time throwing on a pair of soft pajama bottoms. They'd already slept together. He wasn't going to be banished again to his sofa. But he needed the extra barrier between them. He had every intention of finishing what they'd started, but he wasn't going to wake her from a dead sleep to do it. She'd had a few rough nights with Elena. She needed her rest, though if he was going to be noble, he probably should head back to the sofa. His control was tenuous at best.

He slipped into bed, scooting much closer than she'd allow if she were awake. The movement made the mattress dip and Constance let go of his pillow and rolled toward him with a sleepy murmur. He froze. She didn't. She snuggled closer, wrapping her arms around his waist and burying her nose in his neck. It tickled like hell but he held his breath until the urge to laugh and squirm passed. He knew he should wake her, but he was too curious to see what would happen next, not to mention the fact he was thoroughly enjoying himself.

"Luca," she murmured.

Her face tilted upward, searching, but her eyes were still closed. As far as he could tell she was still asleep. She threw a leg over his hip with a little moan and he was a goner. Her lips found his and she pressed closer, rubbing against him. Her tongue darted between his lips and he groaned, rolling her beneath him.

She met his passion with an enthusiasm he'd only caught glimpses of before. They rocked together, hands roving, mouths devouring. And then suddenly she pulled away with a gasp. If she hadn't been awake before, she was now. She looked up at him with bewildered, passion-clouded eyes.

"Hey there," he said.

. . .

Constance took a quick inventory of the situation. She'd been in the middle of the most amazing dream. Then again, judging by the look of things, it hadn't been a dream. She was wrapped around Luca like he was a life preserver, lying half beneath him. Her cheeks stung from the pleasant after effects of an intense make out session with a sexily stubbled man. And the delicious ache building low in her belly left no doubt she'd been enjoying herself immensely.

The rock-hard length of him pressed against her belly, leaving ample evidence of how Luca felt about the whole thing. Now what were they going to do about it? She knew she should pull away. Apologize and retreat back to the other side of the bed, or send him back to his sofa. Or better yet, to a guest room. It was obvious they couldn't be trusted in the same room any longer, let alone the same bed. She had serious doubts, however, about her ability to tear herself away from the mountain of delicious Greek godhood currently poised between her thighs. The thought made her want to scream in frustration. She didn't want to run—she wanted to rip his pants from him and impale herself on the impressive piece of manhood that was currently straining toward her.

"Since when do you wear pants to bed?" she asked, latching onto the most coherent thought in her head.

He chuckled. "You wake up to find us tangled up in the sheets, halfway to the Promised Land, and *that's* what you want to know?"

She smiled and ducked her head, the sudden streak of shyness a bit odd considering her current position. It was now or never. Time to make a decision. Keep running away or give in to what they both wanted. The thought of making herself vulnerable terrified her. But maybe it didn't have to be that way. Luca was...well, he was Luca Vasilakis, heir to one of the biggest real estate moguls in the world. She was a nobody who took care of foster children and orphans. In a couple weeks, their arrangement would be over and they'd both go back to their lives. There was no second-guessing anything. No need to wonder where the relationship was going. She already knew where it was going, which meant she couldn't get hurt. There would be no abandonment down the road because she knew going in exactly when their arrangement would end. If ever there was a time to give in to every woman's fantasy, it was right then. Why shouldn't she seize the moment and do what her body begged her to do?

She squirmed, deliberately rubbing her hips against him. Luca sucked in a ragged breath. "Stanzia, if you're going to walk away, you better do it now."

She looked back into his passion-dark eyes and stroked a hand down his cheek.

"I'm not going anywhere."

That was all he needed to hear. His lips were on hers, their tongues intertwining until they were both breathless. In one smooth movement he had her shirt over her head and on the floor. He paused for a second to gaze at her.

"Aphrodite," he murmured, before bending to suck a tight nipple into his mouth.

She gasped, her hands tangling in his hair to hold him captive. He wrenched away, only to pay homage to the other breast while she writhed beneath him.

"Luca," she whimpered.

He kissed his way down her body, dragging her shorts off as he went down. When she finally lay totally naked before him, he sat back, his eyes shining with admiration and desire.

"You are so unbelievably beautiful," he said. He moved back over her, lightly dragging his body up the length of hers. He'd lost his pants at some point and every exquisite, burning inch of him seared into her body.

"I want to take this slow, but I don't know if I can," he said, moving between her legs.

She shook her head and raised her hips, grinding against him. "We have all night for slow. I want you inside me. Now."

Luca captured her lips again, kissing her until she panted and trembled beneath him. He left her for a brief second to fumble in the drawer beside the bed, coming back with a foil packet. She watched him roll the condom on, inch over delicious inch. He saw her watching and paused, a slow smile stretching over his lips, letting her take in the full vision of him. His black hair brushing his shoulders, those dark eyes burning into hers, knowing exactly what she was thinking, feeling, desiring. His chest, shoulders, and arms rippled with barely contained strength. He could probably tear her apart if he wanted. Instead, those large, warm hands of his trailed down her body so gently, waking every nerve ending, making her crave him.

He loomed over her, his rock-hard abs bunching as he positioned himself over her. Her heart pounded, her body already throbbing for him. She ran her hands over his chest, skimming across his stomach. He sucked his breath in with a hiss and threw his head back. The sight of him so affected by her touch sent a thrill rushing through her. Then he eased into her oh so slowly, retreating only to thrust back in, until he was sheathed inside her as far as he could go. The sensation of him inside her, stretching her to her limit, his rock-solid length caressing the deepest, softest parts of her, made her whimper and tremble.

She wanted to hold still, savor him, relish every thrust, burn the sensations into her memory so she'd never forget how amazing he felt, but the intensity building inside made it impossible. She bucked beneath him, trying to bring him deeper. She ached to touch him. Couldn't get enough of him. His ass seemed made for her hands and she gripped him as she arched into him.

His low growl spurred her on and she rose to meet his thrusts, moving with him. The pleasure building was nothing that she'd ever experienced before. This wasn't just sex. This wasn't some quick fling. He was wrecking her, shattering her, branding her as his.

She tried to increase the tempo but he laughed, low and deep. His hands brushed down her hip and pinned her to the bed. "Hold still, baby. Just let yourself feel. "

He leaned down to nip at her neck, breathe in her ear. "You're already quivering around me. Come on, Stanzia." He thrust into her again, his lips claiming hers, his tongue spearing into her mouth. "Come for me."

Her nails dug into his back. With him holding her down

she couldn't move. It forced her to absorb the pleasure building to a crescendo inside her. Forced her to experience every torturous sensation as he slid in and out, keeping the same steady pace that would drive her to madness.

"Luca!" she gasped, the wave of ecstasy cresting.

He released her, braced himself with his hands on either side of her head, his mouth devouring hers, his tongue plundering. He thrust, hard and deep, his pace increasing until she came, screaming his name. His kiss muffled the sounds of her release as she shuddered and quaked around him.

"God, Stanzia," he said, his body trembling above hers, his rhythm faltering until he came with a roar, pouring his pleasure into her.

He eased himself down and she reveled in his weight resting on her, their heaving breaths mingling, their hearts pounding in time with each other. After a moment he rolled to the side, pulling her with him. He cupped her face and drew her to him for a long, lingering kiss that seared her to her very soul.

It didn't matter anymore what their arrangement was—he could walk away right then and it wouldn't matter. Whatever their deal had been, whatever she'd planned, was no longer valid. She was his. Totally. Completely. And forever. The fact that he probably didn't feel the same was something she'd need to deal with when the time came.

But for her, her entire world had changed, and she had no idea how she'd live in it once Luca was gone.

# Chapter Fifteen

Luca took the remnants of the roll from Constance's fingers and removed the plate with the rest of the desiccated bread from her grasp. Then he took her hands and kissed each one.

"Stop worrying. He's the one who saw that picture of us and decided he liked you, remember? This should be easy."

"Yes, but what if he's changed his mind? We got engaged so quickly. He might think I'm just here for…for…"

"For my money? For a few nights in my bed?" he asked, his voice dropping an octave.

Her breath left her in a gush that left her cheeks flaming red and Luca chuckled, leaning in to kiss her. "I sincerely hope the last one is true."

"Luca," she said, glancing around to make sure no one heard him.

"You have got to relax," he said, with a little laugh.

"Easy for you to say. It's not my father we're about to meet."

"We can do that next. Let's get mine out of the way first."

"You'd want to meet my dad?"

"The man who produced you? Of course. I wanted to meet him before, remember? Not so sure how he'd feel about me…"

Constance laughed. "As long as I'm happy, he'd be happy."

"And are you? Happy?"

He found himself surprisingly anxious to hear the answer to that question. She gazed up into his eyes and opened her mouth to speak but never got the chance.

"Well, look at the happy couple," his father said, staring down at them before taking a seat.

Luca sat back, all playfulness disappearing at his father's disapproving, and unexpected, tone. "Father, I'd like you to meet Constance McMurty. Constance, my father, Augustine Vasilakis."

"It's a pleasure to meet you, Mr. Vasilakis. Luca has told me so much about you."

"Has he? I'm afraid the only things I know about you I had to find out from my investigators."

"Father," Luca said, his tone as close to warning as he'd ever dared get with his father.

"Don't stop on my account," Augustine said, waving a finger between the two of them before unfolding and laying his napkin in his lap. "You want to make sure the photographers you've got clogging up the streets all get a good shot."

Luca frowned, his anxiety turning to anger. "We were not putting on a show for anyone's benefit. Theirs or yours."

"Of course you were," he said, not even bothering to look at Luca. He waved a server over, ordered a glass of wine and sat back to scrutinize them, his gaze lingering on Constance.

"So, you're his *fiancée* at the moment, or so I've heard."

Constance blanched and Luca's anger burned hotter.

"I'm sorry, sir," Constance said, her forehead creased with a small frown. "Have I done something to offend you?"

"No," Luca said. "You haven't."

His father glanced at him, eyebrows raised. "I'm capable of answering for myself, Luca."

The waiter brought his wine but was waved away when he asked if they were ready to order.

"Now, to get back to the question of my offense. Of course I'm offended," he said, but his gaze was on Luca. A small thing to be grateful for in what was apparently going to be a disaster of epic proportions, but if shit was about to get ugly, Luca preferred it fall on him, not Constance. His dad shook his head. "That you would think you could fool me into thinking you've changed by staging some sham wedding, complete with orphans for God's sake, is not only offensive, it's downright infuriating."

"I don't understand where your anger is coming from," Luca said. "You were thrilled when photos first surfaced of us together. Your exact words, I believe, were, 'Finally, a girl your mother would be proud to welcome to our home.' Why the sudden change of heart?"

"I'll admit I was thrilled initially to see you keeping company with someone of a little more substance, for once. But reconciling the son I knew becoming suddenly engaged to a woman with six children to care for was a little more difficult. If you were truly getting married, I wanted to know more about who you were bringing into the family, as any father would.

"My people did a little more digging and discovered that your Miss McMurty here had never once been seen in your presence or anywhere near anyone you associate with until the day those photos were taken. Yet almost immediately, you are engaged, and large donations have been made to the organization she is associated with. I have no idea how much you're paying her on top of the money you've already shelled out, and frankly any woman who would agree to whatever deal you made is reprehensible. But if you think for one second you can bribe and lie your way into my good graces you are sorely mistaken.

"You've made some poor choices in your life, Luca, but even I thought you to be better than this. When will you ever learn that the only way to get ahead in life is to work for it? You can't lie or buy your way into success. You are never going to make anything of yourself this way. And to drag this young woman down into your deceptions with you, though I'm no longer sure considering the behavior I've seen who did the dragging, not to mention using a bunch of innocent children, is nothing short of shameful—"

"That is enough!" Constance slammed her napkin onto the table and Luca and Augustine both looked at her with what he was sure were twin expressions of shock. Mirrored by most of the people in the restaurant. The phones started coming out and Luca was sure within moments their little scene would be all over the internet. Ah well. No help for it. And frankly, the fact that she was defending him was something he was happy to share. No one had ever done such a thing for him before.

He had seen her irritated, even angry, but he'd never seen Constance in full-blown fury. She was magnificent with her flashing eyes and heated cheeks, her chest out and back straight, ready for battle. This might even be fun to watch, especially since it wasn't aimed at him.

He'd listened to his father's tirade with growing anger and a sinking heart, but while things between he and Constance had recently grown a great deal more complicated than he expected, his father wasn't really wrong. How do you argue with that?

Constance was apparently going to try. She stood up, her whole body radiating fury.

"Mr. Vasilakis, I don't know where you get your information, but I assure you nothing about my relationship with your son is false. Yes, it's true that we'd only met that day of the first picture and, yes, we became engaged immediately after. It might have been a whirlwind and it might have been unexpected, for us as well as anyone else, but that does not make it any less real. He proposed, I said yes, he bought me a beautiful ring I will cherish for the rest of my life, and I've been sharing his home, and his bed, ever since."

Luca tried not to look too surprised. She wasn't lying, but she was gilding the truth a bit. He'd never have expected it from his oh-so-proper-Constance.

"To suggest that he has paid me to do any of this is incredibly offensive and you owe me an apology. And you owe your son one as well. Luca might be a bit impetuous and yes, at times he can be irresponsible and maybe even immature…"

Luca's eyes narrowed, wondering where she was going with all that.

"But he is also good, and kind, and loving. He is amazing with my girls. They adore him. If you don't believe that, come see it for yourself instead of sending your flunkies out to Google lies from the internet. Don't you dare accuse him of wrongdoing or berate him like he is some misbehaving child. Luca is a wonderful, decent man who deserves a hell of a lot more credit than anyone ever gives him, and I will not sit by while you belittle and criticize him."

Augustine stared in stunned silence at her and she seemed to realize what she'd just done. Her shoulders slumped a bit, the righteous indignation bleeding out of her bit by bit. She turned to Luca with wide, worried eyes.

He stood and wrapped his arm around her shoulders, pulling her against him so he could kiss her temple.

"I'm sorry," she mouthed to him.

"Shhh," he whispered in her ear. "It's okay. You were incredible."

She looked up at him and he gave her a gentle kiss, briefly resting his forehead against hers.

"Thank you," he whispered, stroking her face. Then he turned to his father, keeping his arm firmly around her. "You may think whatever you like about me, Father. But Constance is off limits. Short of inviting you into our bedroom, there is no way for me to prove anything to you and I have no desire to try. I think we've listened to enough for one day."

He slapped enough euros on the table to cover their bill and took Constance's hand.

"If you'll excuse me, I'm going to take my fiancée home."

His father stood as they left, but he didn't say anything to call them back. If Luca wasn't mistaken, and he could have been since he'd never seen anything like it before, there might have been a look of grudging respect and approval on his old man's face.

Maybe miracles did happen.

They pushed through the doors of the restaurant and were met with a mob of flashing cameras. Constance buried her face against his chest and he wrapped his arm more firmly about her. Reporters started screaming questions at them.

*What did you discuss with your father?*

*Are you fighting with your father?*

*What was the argument about?*

*Does he approve of your marriage?*

*How does he feel about your fiancée?*

*Things looked like they were getting heated in there. Care to comment?*

*Constance! Constance! How does it feel to have Luca's father hate you?*

*Luca! Did he threaten to cut you off if you married Constance?*

*Your fans want to know! Do you have a message to share?*

Yeah…he'd love to tell everyone to fuck off and get out

of their faces, but he refrained. Barely.

Luca shoved through them, for once not worried about trying to make a good impression. Constance trembled under his arm. He needed to get her out of there. They made it to his car and he ushered her in, running around to get in the driver's side. This time, he didn't take it nice and slow so they could get their shots of the happy couple leaving. He revved the engine to serve as warning, lurched forward a foot or two to show he was serious, and then he applied foot to pedal and got them out of there.

They were followed, of course, but they couldn't pass the gates of Luca's estate. He ground to a halt as close to the door as he could get and hurried around to help Constance out of the car.

"I don't feel so well," she murmured.

Her face had gone pale as the white linen dress she wore. Luca wasn't taking any chances. He scooped her up in his arms and carried her inside, ignoring the vultures screeching at them from the other side of the gate.

# Chapter Sixteen

Constance sipped at the water Luca handed her and then put it down, taking a couple deep breaths.

"Thank you. I'm sorry I freaked out. I …I just need a break. I want all this to stop. Just for five minutes. Something." Constance knew she was whining like a two-year-old but she couldn't help it. If one more camera went off in her face, she was going to scream. How the hell did Luca deal with this every day of his life and not go completely insane?

He pulled her into his arms, cradling her head against his chest in a gesture so tender it made her heart twist. Sometimes, most times, he was a total ass, but there were moments like this where a different person seemed to peek out. She sank into him, letting him soothe her. His hands rubbed down her back, his lips moving against her hair as he mumbled in Greek to her, interspersed with kisses so sweet she wanted to cuddle against him and never move.

He tilted her face up so he could meet her gaze, smoothing her hair out of her face. "*Omorfi koritsi mou*," he said, surprising her with the sweet term of endearment. His beautiful girl. It drew a smile from her and she pressed closer to him. He kissed her, his lips gentle, almost chaste.

"Come on," he said, a smile spreading across his face. "Let's get out of here."

Relief flooded through her. "Where are we going?"

"There's a spot I know where they won't find us." He grabbed her hand and pulled her behind him. She had to jog a little to keep up with his long stride.

"What about the kids?"

Luca stopped and pulled his phone from his pocket, quickly firing off a text. He received a response a few seconds later and grabbed her hand again. "They are still at the beach with Joe and Mrs. Ballas. Joe's getting ready to build a bonfire for s'mores. They have them covered for the night. Let's go."

They were in a part of the house she hadn't been in before. Luca pushed open a door and flipped on the lights. They were in a garage, a fully stocked garage. Constance's jaw dropped at the assortment of designer cars and motorcycles neatly lined up on the shining concrete surface of Luca's custom garage. Each vehicle in there probably cost more than she made in a year. What in the world did he need with so many of them on this tiny island?

She gawked at each shiny new specimen, not really noticing where he was leading her until they came to a stop in front of a shiny black and chrome work of art—that Constance would get on over her dead body.

"That's a motorcycle," she said.

Luca's eyebrow rose. "Very good."

"You don't expect me to ride on that thing?" She rode a moped, sure, but that was a little scooter. It was like a toddler's tricycle compared to the massive piece of equipment in front of her.

He pulled a helmet out of a compartment in the back and handed it to her. "Yes, I do."

He kicked a leg over the bike and sat down and somehow that small act made things tighten low and deep in her belly. What the hell was it about a motorcycle that made a man so freaking hot? Luca was insanely attractive to begin with, but sitting with that impressive hunk of machinery between his legs, his jeans taut over his thighs, his shirt doing nothing at all to hide the well-sculpted body it covered made her want to straddle him herself.

She swallowed hard and gripped the helmet in her hands. Luca put his on and held out a hand to her. "Come on, baby. Ride with me."

She pulled the helmet on, feeling ridiculous with the heavy thing balanced on her head. He pulled her closer and helped her strap it on, then tugged on her hand again so she was forced to either slide onto the bike or jump across to the other side.

"Can't we take a car?" she asked, her heart already pounding in her throat.

Luca shook his head. "This is faster and I can take it places I can't take a car. We want to lose the vultures, not lead them to where we're going."

He pulled on her arms and wrapped them around his waist. "Just hold on tight. You'll be fine."

Constance tightened her arms about him and leaned her face against his back. Hmm, this form of transportation did have its benefits, she'd say that much.

Luca kicked the bike on and revved the engine. It vibrated between her legs and Constance gasped, pressing her thighs closer to Luca. She couldn't really hear him over the sound of the bike, but his laughter rumbled against her chest. Okay, so she could definitely learn to enjoy certain aspects of riding the thing.

He hit a button on a control dangling from the keychain and the garage door opened. "Hold on," he yelled back to her.

Before she had a chance to respond, he released the throttle and they were off. She sucked in a breath, squeezed her eyes tight, and held on for dear life. Luca didn't take it slow, either. He flew out of the garage and through the narrow space in the barely opened gate. He must have hit the button again once they were through because when she looked back, everything had started closing. He cranked a hard right onto the main road, and they were gone. She squeezed her eyes shut and held on for dear life.

After a second, once she realized they were still moving and had not died in a ball of twisted fiery metal, Constance opened her eyes and risked a glance behind them. Three of the cars that had been parked in front of the house were following them, photographers hanging out the windows of two of them while their fellows drove.

"There's three of them following us!" she yelled to Luca.

He nodded and patted her hand, squeezing it tight. "Hold on!" he yelled back.

She renewed her grip on him and held on while he weaved in and out of traffic, gunning ahead when no one was in front of them and zooming around anyone who got in their way. The cars behind them kept up for a few minutes but gradually they began to drop back. They couldn't weave around the other cars the way Luca could.

"We're losing them!" she yelled, adrenaline rushing through her.

"Wahoo!" Luca shouted, giving the bike a little extra juice.

The motorcycle flew, pulling ahead of everyone else and finally leaving the congested, narrow streets of town behind them. Constance laughed, and shouted, "Wahoo!" along with him. Exhilaration pumped through her, igniting every cell in her body. The huge machine beneath her still vibrated with power and so did the man between her thighs. Her breath caught in her throat, a wave of desire rolling through her so strongly she moaned aloud.

She pressed closer to Luca. As always, he seemed to know exactly what she wanted. He reached a hand back, dragging it up her thigh, his nails lightly biting into her skin. She gasped again.

"How much farther?" she yelled at the vicinity of his ear.

"We're almost there!"

Thank God, because if he didn't touch her soon she might explode from the pressure building inside. She spread her legs wider, trying to get as close to him as she could without upsetting the delicate balance of the bike. She was wearing a sundress and they were flying over asphalt. The last thing in the world she wanted was to make him wreck, but if he couldn't touch her just yet, maybe she could have a little fun with him. Carefully.

She let her hands trail down his belly until they skirted the band of his jeans. She knew the exact moment he realized what she was going to do. He sat up straighter, every muscle in his body that was pressed so tightly against her tensed and she was pretty sure he held his breath. His back no longer expanded and contrasted with each breath.

She let her hands dip farther until they found the hardening bulge straining against the seam of his jeans. She pressed against him, her fingers caressing the contours of his rigid length. The bike swerved slightly, and she stopped tormenting him so she could renew her death grip around his waist. Okay, so that had been a bad idea. Sort of. Excitement still thrummed through her. She'd never been so alive, so aware.

Luca turned the bike onto a narrow dirt path with trees overhanging so far it was almost impassable. He had to reduce the speed of the bike to a near crawl to get through the growth unscathed. He reached behind him and Constance gasped when his hand gripped her thigh, squeezing it and pulling it slightly over his own leg as far as he could. She draped herself around him, her hands reaching around to find him hard and straining for release.

Her fingers trailed under his shirt, reaching up to caress the hard lines of his abs, tracing every ridge and cord. His hand squeezed her thigh again and then he had to use both hands to keep the bike steady as it crawled down an incline. She pulled her attention away from Luca long enough to see where they were.

A little house, more like a hut really, stood nestled among the trees. Down a short, rocky path, a small expanse of beach stretched before it, the turquoise waves gently lapping at the shoreline. No one else was around. No neighbors. No boats. They were secluded in the beautiful, tiny cove. Constance sighed with pleasure but didn't get a chance to do much more.

As soon as Luca parked the bike and cut the engine, he ripped off his helmet and pulled her around so she sat in front of him, straddling his waist. Everything else on her radar disappeared. Everything but *him*. He yanked her helmet off and then his lips were on hers, his hands cupping her face as their tongues tangled together. She fisted her hands in his hair, dragging him closer, trying to bring him deeper.

She fumbled with his zipper and he reached between them and jerked it down. He grabbed a condom from his back pocket and quickly rolled it on. Then he hooked one of her legs around his hip, yanked her panties to the side, and plunged into her, his mouth muffling her cries.

Oh yes, this is what she wanted, what she needed. She wrapped her other leg around his waist and lifted her hips to meet his thrusts. The pleasure that had been building inside her since the moment he'd kicked the motorcycle on built to a crescendo and her legs tightened around him. One more thrust and she was over the edge, shattering into a million pieces, pulsating around him as he poured his own pleasure into her.

They clung together for a moment, struggling to catch their breath. Constance looked up at him with a shaky laugh. "I've never ridden a motorcycle before. I think I liked it."

Luca's laugh rang out, sending little ripples through her where their bodies were still connected. She sucked in a breath and he leaned down to kiss her again. He stirred inside her again and she pressed closer, wrapped her arms about his neck.

He chuckled again. "Let's take this inside. I want to take my time with the next one."

"Yes, sir," she said.

He quickly adjusted their clothes and then moved off the bike, keeping his arms wrapped around her, holding her in place against him. Thankfully, he didn't seem to mind carrying her in, which was a good thing because she wasn't all that sure her legs were in proper working order just yet.

Once inside, he let her slide down his body until her feet touched the floor. She still didn't let go of him, instead rising on her toes to kiss him. He groaned against her, exploring her mouth until she was breathless and trembling. When he pulled away she gave a little moan of protest. He grinned at her and took her hand.

"Hold on to that thought," he said, pulling her farther into the room. "I want to show you around first."

She gave him a mock pout but followed him into the center of the room. The bungalow was a circular structure, mostly made of the whitewashed stone that prevailed on the islands. A large arched doorway took up one section of the curved space. A tiny kitchen area took up another side. Nothing more than a sink, a short countertop, and a small refrigerator. A door to the left closed off what she assumed was a bathroom. A large, comfortable-looking couch took up the space on the opposite wall. Other than a low coffee table, there was no other furniture in the room.

"There's no bed," she said with a slight frown.

He grinned again and led her to large double wood doors. He pushed them open and she gasped.

"Oh Luca, this is beautiful," she said, pure joy filling her.

The doors opened onto a wood terrace covered with a latticed trellis dripping with vines and flowers. A large circular recliner hung from chains in the center of the terrace. Well, it wasn't a recliner. It was a bed really, or large enough to be one anyway. It reminded her of those DIY shows that took old trampolines and converted them to hanging beds. It was piled high with a soft looking cushion and large, fluffy pillows, and Constance just wanted to jump right in and cuddle down. And steps away, the ocean lapped softly at the tiny sliver of beach that they had all to themselves.

"What is this place?" she asked him, her voice quiet. "It's so peaceful here."

He nodded, his face as relaxed and content as she'd ever seen it as he looked around. "It's my little hideout," he said. "I come here sometimes when I can't stand the circus anymore."

Constance shook her head. "I think I'd stay here all the time. It's amazing."

She bit her lip, briefly wondering how many other women he'd brought here. But she pushed the thought from her mind, not wanting anything to spoil the amazing moment.

"You're the only one I've ever brought here," he said softly.

Constance's gaze shot to his, her eyes widening. "Really?"

He stepped closer. "Not even Joe knows about this place. You're the only one I've ever wanted to share it with."

"Oh, Luca," she murmured, bringing her hand up to caress his cheek.

He wrapped his arms around her waist and began to sway

with her.

She laughed. "What are you doing?"

"Dancing."

"Hmm," she said, draping her arms around his neck. "But there's no music."

He leaned down to gently kiss her. "I don't need music when I'm with you."

Her eyebrow rose slightly. "Are you getting a little corny in your old age?"

"No, Miss McMurty. I believe you are being a disruptive influence on me."

"Oh, I am, huh?" He was being completely silly, but her heart swelled with every word. She liked silly Luca. Hopefully he'd stick around for a while.

"Most definitely." He pulled her in closer. "I haven't had a thing to drink except for that one small glass of wine with dinner last night. I've cleaned up my language. In fact, I can't remember the last time I said a fucking swear word," he said with an impish smile.

Constance's laughter rang out and Luca gave her a delighted grin and continued on with his checklist. "I've worn clean clothes to dinner every night and even washed my hands before sitting at the table, and I haven't been to a proper party in more weeks than I can count. You've turned my life upside down, madam."

"That sounds like quite an ordeal, Mr. Vasilakis. My profound apologies."

"No need to apologize at all, my dear Stanzia. Despite my better judgment, I've enjoyed every moment. Well…maybe not *every* moment. But close."

She smiled, happiness bubbling up from deep within. "I am very glad to hear that my presence hasn't been an undue hardship."

"I didn't say that. It's been downright brutal at times," he said, laughing. "But I think I might be the better for it."

Was it possible to die from happiness? Could she really believe what was coming out of his mouth? She wanted to, desperately. She gazed into his eyes, searched for any sign of subterfuge, for the fake Luca that was on display for the public, but there was no one else there. Just the two of them, no one to put on a show for.

She rose on her tiptoes and kissed his cheek. "Thank you for bringing me here."

In answer, he just smiled and walked backward, gently pulling on her hands. She squinted at him. "Luca, where are we going?"

"It's hot, don't you think? We could use a refreshing swim after our escape from the evil vultures."

She giggled and followed him down the rocky path to the shore, but resisted when he tried to pull her closer to the water. "A swim sounds lovely, but we didn't pack anything. I don't have a bathing suit."

He yanked hard on her hands and she fell against him with a surprised yelp.

"Who says you need a suit?" he said, leering at her.

"I am not skinny-dipping."

"Why not?" he asked, pushing the straps of her dress off her shoulders. "You have beautiful skin, and I want to see all of it." He kissed her collarbone and she stopped trying to pull her straps back up, frozen at the sensations his lips created. "Have you ever been skinny-dipping before?"

"Of course not!" she said, horrified at the thought.

He laughed. "Well, it's far overdue then. You can't imagine how good it feels. With the water touching every inch of you." He pushed her dress farther down. She clasped her arms around her breasts, glancing around in panic.

"There's no one here but us, Stanzia. Just you and me and our own little piece of heaven."

She looked into his eyes, searching him for any hint that he might be teasing her. "You promise me no one can see? There is absolutely no way anyone might stumble on us?"

"I swear to you, my word of honor. I bought this place years ago under a fake name. Like I said, even Joe doesn't know about it. I've never brought anyone else here, ever. I have no neighbors. We're surrounded on all sides by cliffs. No one will see you but me. And I am dying for the sight of you."

He brushed his lips across her shoulders, trailing down to the top of her breasts. She sucked in a breath, her head thrown back to give him better access.

"Come swim with me, Stanzia."

# Chapter Seventeen

Constance looked at Luca, her eyes turned dark with desire. He wanted to see her bathing in the crystal waters of the sea, his own personal Aphrodite. His loins ached with the need for her. But first he wanted to see all of her, touch every inch, worship her from head to toe.

He gave her dress another little tug. This time, she let her arms drop. She kept her gaze on him as he slowly pulled the garment from her and let it drop to the ground. Her panties quickly followed and she was left standing on the shoreline in nothing but the gold sandals he'd bought her.

"You are a goddess, Stanzia," he said, her beauty taking his breath away.

Her cheeks flushed under his scrutiny but she didn't turn or try to hide herself. She stood tall and proud and he wanted to drop at her feet and worship her like they'd done in the olden days.

She kicked off her sandals. "Your turn," she said, a smile tugging at her lips.

He grinned, only too happy to oblige. He whipped his shirt

off and tossed it to the ground, his jeans quickly following. Luca walked backward into the sea, crooking his finger at her to beckon her along. She didn't take her eyes off his, not even when the water lapped over her toes. She shivered a little at the cool touch of the water as it rose up her legs. When it reached the juncture of her thighs, she paused, her mouth dropping open in a little *O* of surprise. He could imagine how the cool water felt hitting her surely overheated sex.

He couldn't resist her anymore. Luca closed the distance between them with one step. He grabbed her around the waist with one hand while the other buried deep in her hair. Her arms wrapped around him and her mouth met his in a desperate kiss. His blood roared, desire for the woman in his arms burning through him. But he wasn't done worshipping her yet.

He dropped to his knees in the surf, the water still gently splashing her. His hands moved up her thighs and slowly spread them apart, giving the sea, and himself, better access. She gripped his shoulders, her body already trembling just from the waves moving against her.

*Oh, baby. You haven't felt anything yet.*

He leaned forward and licked her, his tongue lapping at her heated center in the same gentle motion as the waves. The saltiness from the ocean mixed with her own special taste and Luca delved in deeper. He wanted her to come screaming, so he could feel her quaking against his tongue. His hands gripped her waist even as hers tangled in his hair, imprisoning him against her hungry body. He licked and sucked, gently nibbling at her swollen clit until she arched against him, rocking against his mouth as she sought release. Every few moments he'd retreat, letting the cool waves of the sea wash against her, only to instantly replace it with the heat of his mouth.

Her legs trembled and tensed beneath his hands and he

increased his tempo, mimicking with his tongue what he so longed to do with his body. Her fingers tightened, pulling his hair until he grunted in pain, and she came with a warm rush against his tongue. He caressed her a few more times as the aftershocks swept through her. When she released his hair with a tremulous sigh, he kissed his way up her belly, his lips dancing over her breasts until she quivered against him. "We need to go back to the cottage. I don't have any condoms out here," he said with a gruff laugh.

"I'm still on the pill." She captured his mouth, kissing him greedily.

The thought of being with her with nothing between them nearly brought him to his knees.

She tangled her hands in his hair. "What I want is for you to be inside me. *Now*." Her voice broke off as her breath hitched in her throat.

"Up," he commanded, his voice rough with need.

She didn't hesitate but gripped his shoulders and jumped, wrapping her legs around his waist. He drove into her, groaning as she sheathed him in silken heat one slow inch at a time. When he was fully buried inside her, he waded farther out into the water, deep enough that the water splashed against her tightened nipples as they moved.

He let the waves set their rhythm, pulling back to let the cool water rush between them as they sucked back into the sea and then plunging into her heat as the waves rushed toward the shore. With the desperate edge taken off their lovemaking, he took his time, his gaze burning into hers. They moved together and he captured every moment, every gasp, every delicate flutter of her eyes, every moan. Every detail burned its way into his memory and he knew he'd never be able to be with another woman without remembering this moment. He wasn't all that sure he'd ever be able to be with another woman at all.

Their connection burned with intensity, breaking all the barriers he'd tried to erect, destroying his defenses. She hadn't just gotten under his skin—she'd invaded his heart, his mind. His soul. He'd never be free of her, and he never wanted to be.

With one final thrust, he brought her to climax, screaming his name, her body convulsing around his. Her muscles stroked him, owned him, pushed him over the edge until her name on his lips echoed off the cliffs surrounding their paradise.

She collapsed against him, her body trembling, curling into him. He pressed a kiss to her shoulder and wrapped his arms tighter about her, then carried her out of the water to the waiting bed suspended on the porch. They dropped onto it, their movement setting the bed swinging. Constance giggled, a sweet, lighthearted sound that she didn't make nearly often enough. He sat up long enough to pull the mosquito netting closed. He grabbed one of the soft, furry throws that draped the bed and pulled it up over them.

He kissed her softly, murmuring words in Greek that she probably didn't understand and he didn't want to dwell on. Between their escapades and the gentle swaying of the bed, she was asleep in moments, but Luca remained awake, cradling the woman he loved.

He loved her.

The words seemed alien to him. Impossible. Inevitable.

He'd known the moment he'd walked into his backyard and seen her standing in that storm of childish chaos that she was unlike anyone he'd ever met, and the first time he'd kissed her, he'd known she would change his life. But not even he could have predicted just how much. The fading sunlight glinted off the sapphire ring on her finger and Luca found himself wondering how she'd feel about making their little arrangement permanent, for real.

She'd probably laugh, tell him he was crazy, that it made no sense. They were too different. It was only supposed to be a sham, temporary, that anything more was insane.

The children…that thought still filled him with terror. He wasn't even remotely father material, but maybe with Constance there to help make sure he didn't do any permanent damage, maybe they could make it work. It hadn't been so bad with the kids there these past few weeks. They'd seemed happy. And he…he'd been happy, too.

He brushed her hair from her face and a faint smile crossed her lips, even in sleep. He wrapped himself around her, breathed in her cherry blossom scent.

Yes, it was crazy. But if he was very lucky, she might just say she loved him, too. There was only one way to find out.

But it could wait. For that moment, he was content to hold her. For the rest, he'd suck it up and do what terrified him the most. He'd bare his soul and hope she didn't reject it.

Tomorrow.

. . .

Constance woke early, the morning sun gently stealing across the beach to reach them in their swinging nest. She sighed happily, reaching out for Luca only to find he was no longer beside her. Her movements set the bed swinging when she sat up, so she took care when she climbed down. She wrapped a blanket around her, following the sound of Luca's voice.

He stood outside the front door, already dressed, speaking on the phone. She couldn't hear his words but by his tone he was obviously displeased about something. He must have heard her step because he turned to glance at her. He frowned, not aiming it at her but at something he must be hearing, then he turned back around.

A deep unease settled in her gut. This was not the way she expected the morning to go. After the night before…he'd been so loving. That hadn't just been lust and sex; it had meant something. To her at least. And to him, she'd been sure of it.

He put his phone back in his pocket and came inside.

"Is everything okay?" she asked.

Luca frowned again. "Nothing that can't be handled."

He gave her a strained smile that did little to ease the ache settling in her heart. "We're going to have to cut our morning short. There are a few things I need to take care of. I'd like to leave in a few minutes if possible."

She nodded, her throat suddenly tight. "Probably best," she managed to say. "I'm sure Mrs. Ballas could use a break by now."

He caught her hand before she could turn around and pulled her to him.

"I'm sorry," he murmured, leaning down to press a sweet kiss to her lips. "This isn't how I wanted our morning to go."

"Me, either," she said with a small smile.

He wrapped her in his arms, hugging her close for a few moments. Then he kissed the top of her head and sent her toward the bathroom with a playful slap to her rear. He was trying. Too hard, maybe. Something was definitely wrong.

She dressed as quickly as she could, the mood of their idyllic getaway tarnished with whatever he was keeping from her. When she came out, he was pacing the room, running his hands through his hair.

"Hey," he said, grabbing her hands and drawing her in for a kiss. "What do you say to a trip?"

"A trip? Where? I mean…I'd love to, but I can't leave the kids…"

"For all of us. You, me, and the kids. Mrs. Ballas can come along to help wrangle."

Constance still sensed an underlying tension to him, but he did seem genuinely excited about his plan.

"Where would we go?"

"I've told Joe to get the yacht ready. We can cruise around

the islands, get away from everything for a while, all the craziness. It can just be us."

"That sounds wonderful. Can you do that? I mean, aren't you supposed to meet with your dad again soon?"

"Don't worry about him. This isn't about him anymore. This is about us." He cupped her face and drew her in for a kiss.

She sank into him, letting the last of her anxiety drift away. Whatever had upset him earlier didn't seem to be an issue. She'd probably blown it out of proportion.

"Let's go home and get packed," he said, breaking away long enough to gather up the rest of the things they'd brought.

"What, you mean we're leaving today?"

"Why not? You didn't have any other plans, did you?"

"Well, no." Constance laughed. "I guess I'm not used to having someone say *hey let's go on a cruise in my yacht* and have it be an actual possibility."

He grinned. "Well, get used to it." He gave her a quick kiss and then pulled her out the door to the motorcycle.

She wrapped her arms around him again but tried not to get too carried away. They'd be walking into a house with six kids this time, not a private bungalow. They might not be able to rush straight to the bedroom upon arrival.

When they pulled up to the house, however, the kids were nowhere to be seen. The house was almost eerily quiet.

"I wonder where everyone is," Constance said.

Joseph came out of Luca's office. Constance gave him her usual bright smile but his expression was tight, subdued. What was going on?

Luca frowned at Joseph and wrapped his arm around Constance's waist. "Is everything ready?"

Joseph nodded. "She'll be ready to leave within the hour."

"Excellent." Luca turned to Constance. "As soon as you can get packed we'll head over."

"So quickly?"

"Why wait?" he said, though the smile he gave her seemed forced.

"Luca, what's going on?"

"Can't a man want to take his fiancée and a parcel of kids on a trip without something being wrong?" he asked with a spark of his usual humor.

She relaxed a little. "I suppose."

"Then go pack your bags so we can get this show on the road."

"Yes, sir," she murmured, leaning in for a kiss that was so sweet and gentle it raised red flags all on its own.

She pulled away with a slight frown. "Luca…"

He cupped her face in his hands. "There are several things we need to talk about, Stanzia, but I don't want to do it here. I want to get you and the kids on my boat and get underway so we can relax and take our time."

"Am I going to like what you have to say?" she asked, not sure if she should be excited or terrified. Surely he wouldn't be planning a trip with her if he were going to break things off. She couldn't imagine anything more awkward than being stuck on a boat with someone you'd dumped, with six kids you had no real tie to tossed in for fun.

"I hope so," he said, pulling her closer for another kiss that curled her toes and melted her heart. "Now go get packed."

She grinned and hurried off to their room to grab her things.

She had her bag nearly ready to go when Mrs. Ballas came in.

"Oh, Mrs. Ballas, good. I was wondering where you and the children had gotten to. Are they packed and ready to go?"

"They're all ready, but I wanted to make sure you really wanted to go before I told them where we were going. No sense in getting them excited if they weren't going to get to go after all."

Constance frowned. "Of course we're really going. Why wouldn't we?"

"I thought you might be upset over what was in the papers this morning. I suppose that's why Mr. Vasilakis is taking you on a trip. It's a good idea, actually, get away from it all until those jackals find some other bones to chew on."

The knot reformed in Constance's stomach. She didn't want to ask, didn't want to know. There shouldn't be anything in the papers. Nothing new, anyway. Nothing Luca would feel the need to take her away from. They hadn't been anywhere but his bungalow. Maybe they'd gotten some unflattering pictures of her on the beach earlier?

"I don't know what you're talking about, Mrs. Ballas. What's in the papers this morning?"

The old woman's eyes widened in surprise. "Oh. I'm sorry. I thought Mr. Vasilakis would have told you. I shouldn't have said anything."

"Mrs. Ballas," she said, trying to hold her temper, but the panic rising in her throat was making that more difficult by the second. What could be so bad that Luca would want to take her away? "Please just tell me what is going on."

Mrs. Ballas frowned, but she nodded. "Not right, you not knowing. Mrs. Lasko showed me this morning. There are pictures today. All over. Of…well…you and Mr. Vasilakis…" Her face flamed red and Constance's stomach dropped.

Either some enterprising photographer had managed to get a picture of them in their bedroom or…or there had been one at Luca's supposedly secret bungalow. The one no one knew about where they would be perfectly safe and private, and free to make love on the private beach and on the private porch bed.

She'd been such a colossal fool. He had to have set it up. No one could have followed him with his crazy antics and backtracking on that motorcycle. Oh God. What if they'd gotten pictures of them on the motorcycle in front of the bungalow? Why would he do that? He had more than enough images of them together. Why set her up like that? Let the vultures take pictures of their most intimate moments just to prove that their relationship was real? What a joke! Even she'd started to believe it. No wonder he wanted to whisk her away on a yacht where she wouldn't see any newspapers or magazines, where internet connections would be spotty and she'd be too busy basking in the lap of luxury to pay attention to what was going on in the outside world.

His distance that morning made sense now. He'd finally gotten what he wanted, undeniable proof that they had a full relationship in every way. His father had questioned it and now he could see for himself.

She swallowed hard against the tears that choked her. She wouldn't cry over him. He wasn't worth her tears. "Mrs. Ballas," she said, glad when her voice came out steady and calm. "Please get the girls ready to leave. We'll be going back to our own home. I'd like to leave as soon as you can manage."

Mrs. Ballas nodded, thankfully not questioning their sudden change of plans. "They were already packed for the trip. I'll have them gather the rest of their belongings."

"Thank you. Please get everything loaded into the van. I'll join you in a few minutes."

The old woman patted her kindly on the arm. "You deserve better, my dear."

Constance had no response for that so she merely nodded.

Did she deserve better? She'd gone into this crazy relationship knowing full well what it was. She'd slept with him of her own free will. He hadn't coerced her into it, unless you counted being inhumanely sexy as coercion. He'd never told her he loved her. Perhaps she'd read too much into all the lingering glances, soft kisses, and sweet, tender lovemaking.

Maybe all it boiled down to was a man who was really good in bed and a woman who was too lonely and desperate to realize good sex was all it was.

He had no right to splash intimate images of them all over the world. She covered her face, tears burning her eyes at the sudden realization her father would see those photos. The Reverend Mother would see. Would they take the children from her? Yes, the world thought she and Luca were engaged, but they weren't yet married. There were some things even someone as tolerant as the Reverend Mother couldn't overlook.

How could he do this to her? Why?

# Chapter Eighteen

Luca paced in his office, more furious than he'd ever been in his life. Anger burned its way through him, making his blood boil. The only thing keeping him from smashing his fist into every wall of the house was the desire to get the hell out of town as quickly as possible. He had no time for a trip to the hospital for broken bones.

He would sue every publication that had run the pictures. The damn paparazzi had been invasive before, but this took it to a level of depravity even he hadn't anticipated. They should have been safe at his bungalow. No one knew where it was. Yes, he'd originally planned for photographers to shoot them that night, but not there, and he'd called it off.

He pinned his gaze back on Joe, who for the first time in the ten years they'd worked together actually looked flustered.

"I told you to call off all other photo ops."

"I did, sir. Before we'd even left the beach. All scheduled sessions were canceled. Even had that not been the case, I don't see how they could have known where you'd be. The photographers had been told you'd be at the Mykonos Grand last night, and as I suspected, quite a few of them showed up anyway. I don't know how they'd have known where to find you. Perhaps you were followed?"

Luca frowned. "It's possible, though I don't see how. Besides, some of these pictures were taken moments after we arrived. They would have had to be there waiting already. There is only one way in and out of that place. If they'd come up the road, we would have seen or heard them."

"The only explanation is that someone must have tipped them off," Joe said, a frown creasing his brow.

"That's not possible. Mrs. Lasko hires different people to clean the place whenever I need it and takes care of stocking the place for me. No one she brings in knows who I am. I purchased it under a false name, and they never know when I'm going to arrive."

"Drones, maybe?"

"Possible, I suppose." He whirled back around with a growl and resumed his pacing.

If he found out someone had tipped them off…he really couldn't be held responsible for what he'd do.

He never should have brought Constance back to the house. They should have gone straight to the yacht. His only hope was to get her away, convince her that his feelings for her were genuine, that he truly cared for her and would never do anything to hurt her. Maybe then she'd believe that he had nothing to do with this.

The moment she walked into his office, he knew it was too late. Her pain-filled eyes bore into his, fury radiating from her.

"Joe," he said quietly. He didn't take his gaze from Constance, just trusted that Joe would know what he wanted. The quiet click of the door announced that they were alone.

"Stanzia," he began, but she didn't let him finish.

"How could you?" Her voice was a harsh whisper that tore into his heart.

"I didn't do this."

"I don't believe you."

That brought him up short. He'd known she'd need some convincing. He expected confusion and hurt, certainly, but he *hadn't* expected wholescale accusation right off the bat. It hurt much more than he'd expected.

"I want to see them," she said, folding her arms across her chest.

He thought about saying no. He didn't want her to see them. Didn't want her to know the level someone had sunk to in order to make a buck, but she'd see them anyway. They were everywhere.

He went to his computer and pulled up the screen he'd been looking at. Six tabs were open to some of the biggest sites. All had their pictures splashed across the screen with nothing but a few little black bars or blurred pixels to keep the photos publishable. She kept her eyes on him as she walked to his side of the desk. He stepped back with a resigned sigh. There was no stopping the disaster now. He could only hope she'd hear him out.

Her eyes dropped to the screen, her face flushing as she read the bold headlines streaked across every page.

REAL AFTER ALL!

LUCA'S LOVE NEST!

LUCA'S LADY IS A TRAMP!

Some of the others weren't as tame, or kind, but it was the pictures that caused the whimper of distress emanating from her lips. He tried to put an arm around her waist but she pushed him away as she scrolled through picture after picture.

Her, arching back on his motorcycle, her legs wrapped around his waist, her black-barred breasts thrust into the air.

Him, on his knees before her, his face buried against her,

her head thrown back in ecstasy.

Her, wrapped around him in the sea, staring into his eyes as they made love.

For the last time.

He knew it before she said a word.

She stumbled back from the computer. "These…are everywhere?"

He nodded, his heart sinking. Her eyes darted around, searching for something. Not him. Her gaze landed on him and she recoiled like she'd been struck.

"This is a nightmare," she said, her voice thick with tears. "This can't be real. This can't be what my life has been reduced to. I want to wake up and be plain old anonymous Constance McMurty again."

"Stanzia, I'm so sorry. I don't know how—"

"Of course you know how," she said, fury replacing the pain in her face. "This is all your fault, it must be. You swore up and down that no one knew where we were. No one knew about that place. There was no way we were followed. So if all that's true, then you are the only one who could have tipped off the press. You're the one with everything to gain from this."

"Gain? What can I possibly gain from this?"

"Are you serious?" she asked, nearly shrieking. "You were the one worried that people might think we were a sham. You were the one wanting a way to prove to everyone we were the real deal. Well, there you have it, proof that you really were screwing me."

He flinched. "I never wanted this. I would never have condoned someone taking pictures of us in our private moments."

"That's all you've done since the day I met you. Tried to figure out ways to orchestrate being photographed in our private moments, and you are the only one who could have orchestrated *this*!"

"I didn't," he said, trying not to shout, trying to rein in his anger and panic enough to convince her of the truth. She was slipping from his fingers right before his eyes and he didn't think there was any way he could stop it.

"You aren't the only one spread out naked for the whole world to see, Stanzia. I'm on that bike with you. I'm on that beach, too. Yes, I wanted the world to believe we were truly engaged, but the reason I needed that was to convince my father that I had changed and could be an asset to the company. Do you really think splashing around naked pictures of myself making love to you would be the way to accomplish that?"

"Why not? Look at the articles," she said, jabbing her finger at the screen. "I'm the tramp, you're the stud. Our engagement looks real and you come out the winner, like you always do. Is there even one woman on your father's board? I guarantee the only thing the men will do is high five you. Once again, you claim to despise what the media is doing but you reap all the benefits."

He jammed his fingers through his hair, the effort to keep from screaming overwhelming. "What benefits? I don't care about my father's company or what the board thinks or anything else. All I care about is you and all this has done is made you hate me."

She threw her hands up. "It's easy to say that now when you've already gotten everything you wanted. You might say you don't like your privacy being invaded, but this won't actively hurt you. Don't you get that?" Her chest heaved with the force of her words and the tears that she had kept at bay until that moment slipped down her cheeks. He wanted to take her in his arms, brush them away.

"This," she said again, waving her hand to encompass all the media on his desk. "In the long run, this won't hurt you. You have definitive proof we were together."

The "were" hit him like a fist to the gut, but she wasn't

done yet.

"You're a man. You're a hero, a stud, someone to be congratulated, not mocked and scorned. Even if this doesn't help you with your career, it won't hurt you. But for me...I take care of my girls. I have to report to the church." A sob escaped her throat and she slapped a hand over her mouth as the tears flowed.

"I might lose them all. Do you realize that? They might take my girls from me because of this, and they'll never let me adopt Elena now. It was a long shot before, but even if I wasn't married or rich, I still showed exemplary character. No one could reproach my actions, but now...now I might lose everything. Whether you tipped them off or not, you invited them in. You made them a part of our relationship to make yourself look better. We only *had* a relationship for the press. And it worked for you so don't tell me that this affects you, too. Don't stand there and act like this will hurt you. You dragged me into this circus with you and you've destroyed my life."

Every word she flung at him chipped another piece from his heart. The bitch of it was, she wasn't wrong. Every one of the articles had praised him for his virility, even those that shook a finger at him, even as they'd slammed her. Shamed her. Mocked her.

"I won't let you lose the girls," he said, at a loss for what he could say to make this better, but wanting to do something to assure her.

She shook her head and wiped her eyes. "Money doesn't fix everything, Luca."

He looked at her, his chest aching like his heart was being squeezed in a vice. "I didn't know you wanted to adopt Elena."

"What difference does that make now?"

She shook her head again and took off her ring, laying it on his desk. Then she turned toward the door.

"Stanzia…" he called, his hand stretched out to stop her.

"Don't follow me, Luca. You've done enough."

He dropped his hand and watched her walk away.

The front door closed and he slumped into the chair behind his desk.

The house was silent. He was alone, with nothing but a stack of pictures to show that she'd been in his life at all.

# Chapter Nineteen

"Sir?" Joe poked his head in the door and Luca dragged his attention away from the picture he held.

"What is it, Joe?"

He entered the room and clasped his hands behind his back. "I have discovered who has been leaking your whereabouts and personal information, sir."

Luca's gaze shot to Joe's. "What? Who?"

Joe straightened his shoulders like he was preparing for a fight. "Before I tell you, I'd ask that you hear her out. Obviously, what she did was grievously wrong, but there were extenuating circumstances, one could say…"

Luca stood, his hold on his anger tenuous at best. Whoever the leak was had cost him Constance. Forgiveness wasn't foremost in his mind, and neither was patience. "Joe."

That one word held all his frustration and anger and grief and Joe knew it. He nodded his head and went to the door.

Mrs. Lasko walked in, her hands clutched so tightly together they were turning white.

Luca was so stunned he dropped back into his chair.

"What's going on here?"

Mrs. Lasko looked up at Joe. He gave her a small nod and then turned to Luca. "Mrs. Lasko is your leak."

"I gathered that." He looked at the woman he'd trusted with his life, and love. "Why?" he said, his voice not much more than a whisper and all the more terrifying for it if the sudden blanching of Mrs. Lasko's face was any indication.

"My granddaughter," she said, her voice thick with tears. "I thought you had hurt my granddaughter. I was so angry that you would do such a thing. So I thought, I can't do much, but…"

Luca held up his hand. "I've never met your granddaughter, Mrs. Lasko, and I'd certainly never hurt her."

She glanced up at Joe and he patted her shoulder and took over. "Mrs. Lasko's granddaughter is Maria, the maid that comes in to clean twice a week."

A twinge of shame squirmed through Luca at the realization that he hadn't even known the name of the woman he'd seen coming in with Mrs. Lasko to clean, let alone that she was the granddaughter of his trusted housekeeper.

"Maria fell in love with, as she told her grandmother, her employer."

Luca's eyebrows rose in surprise but Joe hurried on before he could speak. "She also told Mrs. Lasko that her employer had returned her love, but then had left her brokenhearted. She naturally assumed it had been you."

Luca snorted. "Naturally."

"But…it was, in fact…" Joe cleared his throat and…was that a blush on his cheeks? Luca sat forward, starting to enjoy the little show taking place before him.

"It was me, sir."

"Joe? You devil."

Mrs. Lasko looked between the two of them probably much as Luca had. Torn between laughing, crying, and wanting to hit someone in the head with a nice heavy object.

"So, let me get this straight," Luca said, sitting forward to clasp his hands on his desk. "Joe here was dating your granddaughter, broke up with her, and broke her heart, and when she told you it had been her employer, you assumed it was me. So to get revenge, you were the one leaking all the personal stuff to the press."

Mrs. Lasko nodded her head. "I'm so very sorry, Mr. Luca, but I love my granddaughter. And I thought…"

He held up his hand again. "I understand. It's all right, Mrs. Lasko. You may go."

A tear trailed down the old woman's face and she nodded her head. "I'll gather my things."

"You misunderstand me," Luca said. "You may go back to your duties. I'd like to talk with Joe for a minute."

She looked up at him, stunned. He was rather surprised himself, but the old woman had been with him for years. He couldn't imagine his home without her, and he couldn't particularly blame her for the misunderstanding or how she'd handled it.

"Yes, sir," she squeaked out with a smile.

"If one more thing gets leaked to the press…"

"No, no, no, sir. No more. I know it wasn't you now." She turned a not-so-friendly glance on Joe and then hurried out the door.

Luca sat back and shook his head. "Well, well. What kind of mess have you gotten yourself into?"

Joe actually looked embarrassed. Luca couldn't remember a time when Joe had ever been less than totally put together and in control of the situation. He hated to admit how much he was enjoying their positions being reversed for once.

"I apologize that my personal issues have affected your life."

Luca nodded. "That they have. Can I ask why you broke up with the young lady?"

Joe grimaced. "I'm sorry to say it was because I didn't want to leave you."

Luca's eyebrows hit his hairline. "What have I got to do with all this?"

Joe pointed at the chair across from the desk and Luca nodded his permission. "She started hinting at wanting to get married."

"And you didn't want to?"

"On the contrary, I'd consider myself the luckiest man in the world to marry her."

"Then what's the problem?"

"I live here, sir. I work for you, sometimes twenty-four hours a day. I couldn't do that if I had a wife. We'd have to find our own place and…"

"Why?" Luca asked.

"Sir?"

"I'll agree that you wouldn't be able to work for me twenty-four hours a day if you were married. It wouldn't be fair to your wife. But then working that much for me isn't all that fair to you, either, is it?"

"I enjoy working for you, sir."

"Glad to hear it. I hope you continue to work for me for a long time to come. However, that does not mean you can't have your own life. The guesthouse in the back is empty. It's yours if you want it."

Joe's jaw dropped. "Sir…I couldn't…"

"Of course you can. You live on the property anyway. Now you'll just have a little more space. Plenty, I should think, to bring along a wife."

"Yes, plenty, sir."

"And I'll work on needing you a little less."

Joe laughed at that. "I'll believe that when I see it, sir."

Luca snorted again. "I said I'd *try*."

Mrs. Lasko knocked on the door again and entered with

a package. "This just came for you, sir."

"Thank you, Mrs. Lasko." She nodded and went out, her steps light, a hum on her lips. Well, at least someone was happy because he was pretty sure his day was about to go from bad to seven circles of hell worse.

He took the package and opened it, his heart already sinking. Another gift for Constance returned. This one he'd been sure she'd keep. He'd chosen it with special care and she'd just sent it right back. He couldn't even tell if she'd opened it and seen what it was. He slammed the diamond locket in its velvet box into the trash with a curse. Joe fished it out and calmly laid it on his desk. It made Luca want to throw it away again.

"I don't know what the damn woman wants!" he shouted, shoving his hand through his hair and nearly pulling out a few stands in his frustration.

"I don't think Miss Constance wants anything, sir."

Luca scowled. "I know that. I just meant I don't know what will make her happy. I've apologized, over and over. I've sent her flowers, jewelry, even first edition books from that god-awful author she loves so much. I've shown up on her doorstep and begged. Nothing works. She's sent me away and returned everything I've sent. What's it going to take?"

"To make her happy? Or to make her forgive you?" Joe asked.

Luca stopped pacing and stared at him. He'd hit the nail on the head, as usual. Luca dropped into his chair. He'd waited a whole two days before he'd started his campaign to win Constance back. That had been a month ago and she hadn't caved one inch. She'd refused to see him, and standing on her porch begging her to talk to him upset her, which upset the children, so he'd stopped showing up in person. But she'd sent back every gift he'd sent, wouldn't answer his texts or emails. He'd even resorted to sending an actual letter through the mail. It had been returned unopened.

"I don't know what to do, Joe. I know I should probably let it go, leave her alone like she's asked. But I…can't. I need her…maybe it really is too late."

Joe watched him for a minute and then sat down in the chair in front of the desk. Luca glanced at him, startled. He couldn't remember the last time Joe had sat without Luca forcing him to.

"May I speak frankly?"

Luca nodded. "Of course."

"You've been trying to win Miss Constance back by doing what you'd like. Or what other women in your past have wanted. Miss Constance isn't like anyone else."

A hint of a smile touched Luca's lips. "No, she's not."

"She didn't love you because of your money."

Luca's gaze shot up again. "You think she loved me?"

Joe gave him an indulgent smile, the type a father would give a son who'd finally figured out how to tie his own shoes. "Yes, sir. She did. I think she still does, but you won't win her back by throwing money at her. She doesn't care about your money. She never did."

Luca frowned and rubbed his chin, thinking. No. She'd had fun with some of the things his money provided, but it wasn't what she'd cared about.

"If I want to show her I love her, I need to show her I care about the things *she* loves."

Joe nodded. Luca rubbed at his eyes, despair filling him. "Maybe it won't even matter. Even if she forgives me, she won't come back and I can't blame her for that. I can't make the vultures stop swarming. They'll always be there, taking pictures, hounding her and the kids. What kind of life would I be asking them to share? No matter what I can give her, how much I love her, it's not worth it. She and the girls deserve a better man than me. I'm not what they need."

"I think you sell yourself short, sir."

Luca snorted and shook his head. "Not something I'm often accused of."

Joe gave him a sad smile. "An unfortunate shortcoming in your life, sir. You're a good man. A little misguided, perhaps. Immature at times. Impetuous. Arrogant. A bit spoiled."

Luca cocked an eyebrow. "Where are you going with this, Joe?"

Joe cocked his head. "Miss Constance and her girls need a good man who loves them. That's all. Everything else will work itself out. And whatever else you are, sir, you *are* a good man. Who loves them."

Luca pulled the jewelry box toward him and opened it. Inside lay a diamond and platinum locket. He popped it open and gazed at the picture of Constance and Elena he'd had placed inside. He rubbed a thumb across their images.

"Will it be enough?" he asked quietly.

"I think those seven special ladies need someone to love them more than anything, sir. If you love them, it will be enough."

Luca stood, hope flickering in his heart again. Faintly, but it was enough.

"What's the plan, sir?"

Luca grinned at Joe. "I'm going to show her that I care about the things she cares about, that my life can be about more than photographers and fame. I'm going to do what I can to make my world a safe place for her and the girls, and then I'm going to win her back."

• • •

Constance fiddled with the embroidery on her dress while she waited for the Reverend Mother to come in. It had been three months since she'd sat in that office waiting to see if Luca would show up. She flinched away from using his name, even in her head. After all these months, she'd hoped life would return to normal, that she'd forget him, or at the very least that the memories would have faded so the mere mention of him didn't strike her like a stab to her heart.

But they hadn't faded. She still dreamed of him almost every night. She still woke in the morning, her heart and body aching from missing him. He'd done what he promised; he hadn't let her lose her girls. Constance didn't know how much he'd donated to the organization, but it was enough for them to overlook anything that had occurred and keep her on as a House Mother.

It wasn't enough to erase those images from the internet. But he'd been right. After a while, other scandals had risen to take their place. They'd never go completely away. Some idiot would post one every now and then. But for the most part, it was as if Luca had never been in her life.

After several shots of her without her engagement ring, they'd finally gotten the hint that she and Luca were no longer together. She'd kept close to home, only venturing out when necessary. Eventually, the press had decided she was boring and no longer relevant and had left her alone.

The odd thing was that Luca had also apparently dropped off the face of the earth. She knew he'd been in London and New York. There'd been shots of him, looking heartbreakingly handsome in a tailored suit, going into his father's office building. A few of him buying coffee. Walking down the street glowering at the cameras. But no parties. No clubs. No women hanging on his arm.

Constance was grateful for that last one, even if she had no claim on him. Still, in the first few weeks especially, it would have killed something in her to see him move on so quickly. Not that there had been anything to move on from. Their relationship hadn't been real. They were both free to find other people, or so she kept telling herself.

He'd tried contacting her a few times in those first few weeks. He'd sent her flowers, signed books, even an exquisite diamond and platinum locket with a picture of her holding Elena that day on the beach. That one had been hard to send back. It wasn't only gorgeous but an incredibly thoughtful gift that had broken another little piece of her heart, but she couldn't accept it. And he'd stopped trying.

That was a good thing. It needed to happen so they could both go on with their lives. But she'd still cried herself to sleep the night she'd realized she wouldn't hear from him again.

The office door opened and the Reverend Mother came in. She waved Constance back into her seat when she stood and Constance perched on the edge of her chair, her legs bouncing, her nerves getting the better of her.

The older woman sat behind her desk, folded her hands, and sat looking at Constance for what seemed like forever. Finally, she asked, "How have you been doing?"

Constance blinked, taken aback for a second. She'd been brought in so they could ask her how she was?

"I'm fine, thank you."

Reverend Mother's lips pursed and she looked over the rim of her glasses at Constance. "Mrs. Ballas tells me you don't leave the house unless you must. And that you've changed in other ways."

Mrs. Ballas needed to keep her mouth shut.

"I haven't noticed that I stay at home any more than usual, or that I've changed."

Reverend Mother did that over-the-rim look again. "Come, child. You are pale, and look as though you don't sleep well, and the laughter is gone from your eyes. You have lost your joy, I think."

Constance opened her mouth to protest that but was horrified to find tears flooding her eyes instead.

"I'm sorry. I know it's wrong."

"Why is it wrong?"

Constance frowned. "Because he…he and I…our relationship…" She took a deep breath and decided to just come clean. It made no difference now anyway.

"Everything about our relationship was a lie. Our engagement was a sham, a publicity stunt for him to get back into his father's good graces, and for me to get back into yours after the girls trespassed on his property while under my care. And then, well, then those pictures…"

Her blood pulsed through her cheeks, setting her face on fire.

"Yes," the Reverend Mother said drily. "Those were unfortunate, I'll grant you that."

Constance kept the sarcastic remark that popped into her head to herself.

"However," she continued. "I saw something in the other pictures taken of you before that incident that I found to be more interesting."

Constance frowned. "The other pictures?"

The Reverend Mother placed several magazines on the desk and pushed them toward her. A new wave of pain washed over her and Constance bit her lip to keep from crying out. She hadn't even known some of those pictures had been taken. There was one of her and Luca at a restaurant, holding hands and laughing. One of them walking along a sidewalk, smiling at each other. The ones that really struck her hard were the ones of their last day on the beach with the girls.

Luca with his arms around her waist from behind, his cheek caressing her upturned face.

Luca watching as she cradled and rocked Elena, a look of such tenderness on his face that Constance's throat grew tight. She hadn't even known he'd been watching.

Luca with a look of gentle wonderment cradling Elena

while she slept.

"You know what I don't see here?" the Reverend Mother asked.

Constance looked up and shook her head, afraid if she spoke, she'd cry.

"I don't see a sham relationship."

Constance's mouth dropped open. She wanted to protest, insist that it hadn't been real, but it had felt real. Everything about it, almost from the first moment, had felt real.

"I see two people who love each other and who love that little girl. He might have said the photos were for publicity, but this," she said, pointing at a close-up of Luca's face as he gazed into hers, "this isn't imitation. He's not that good an actor."

That surprised a laugh out of Constance.

"And neither are you, my dear."

Constance took a deep breath and ducked her head, unable to look the other woman in the eye when she said, "I'm not. I do love him."

A triumphant sigh came from the Reverend Mother. "I thought so."

"But that doesn't matter."

"Why not?"

"How can I ever trust him? He has this weird love-hate relationship with the press. He hates them, but he can't stay away. It's like he's driven to act in a way that will keep him in the spotlight. I can't live like that. I can't subject the girls to that. I don't want to be used to keep him in the papers. I don't want any part of that, and if it came down to his fame or me... well, I've already seen what he'll choose."

"Have you? What did he say when those pictures came out?"

Constance took a deep breath and blew it out. She'd shied away from any thought of that day in his office. "He said it wasn't his fault, that he didn't know how they'd found us."

"And you didn't believe him?"

She thought about it, had been thinking about it since she'd walked out his door. "I don't know. My gut says no, he wouldn't do that. He'd do a lot…but he wouldn't have let photographers be there for something so private."

"Well then…"

"Yes, but what if I'm wrong?"

"Then you are wrong. There aren't any guarantees in this life, Constance, about anyone or anything."

"I suppose that's true."

"Do you know what he's been doing since you left him?"

Constance frowned. "No. After the first few weeks…no. He hasn't really been in the papers or anything."

"Doesn't that show you he's already changed?"

"Maybe." Constance wanted to believe. Desperately. Wanted to think he could change, live away from the spotlight, live as normal a life as possible. He'd never be completely normal, of course, but there was a difference between being famous and being infamous. And until recently, Luca had been on the wrong side.

"I have been informed of at least one thing he's been doing over the last few weeks. I think you will be pleased. That is actually the reason I brought you in today. He will be on television tomorrow to make his grand announcement. He asked me to meddle a bit and try to be sure you'd watch."

The thought of seeing Luca again, even on television, made Constance's stomach flip in excitement and fear. It had taken her weeks to be able to see his face in a magazine without wanting to cry. And that was when she saw him by accident. Purposely tuning in to watch him live on television might be more than she could take. But curiosity was going to get the better of her.

"All right. I'll watch."

And hopefully by the time it was over, she'd still be sane.

# Chapter Twenty

Luca straightened his tie for the hundredth time and smoothed his hands down his tailored shirt. Joe helped him with his jacket, pulling at the shoulders, picking off imaginary lint. He'd been fidgeting all morning, unable to sit still, but he didn't want to pace the room like some caged tiger, so he sat on the couch in the studio's green room, waiting for his segment to be announced.

Someone with a headset popped her head in and said he was up in five minutes. Luca nodded and straightened his tie again.

"Did you give them the list of topics to stay away from?" he asked Joe for probably the fourth time.

Patient as always, Joe answered, "Yes, sir. They will ask about your new project only and will not talk about your engagement or former fiancée or anything else of a personal nature."

"Good." He hoped the Reverend Mother had been able to convince Constance to watch today. He wanted her to see what he'd been working on, but he had no intention or desire to go out there and spread more of their personal details around the world, especially if she was watching.

He was done with that, done with the fans and the media and the fame and all of it. He'd thrown himself into his work after Constance had left. His father had finally been convinced that even without her he'd made a change for the better. Grown up. He'd been given control of the New York offices, a move that, in his mind, allowed him to do something worthwhile with his life for once. Maybe someday he could convince Constance that what they'd had was real, and worth giving a second shot.

He took his place behind the curtains and waited for his introduction. When he was announced he went out, smiling and waving for the cameras. He took a seat on the couch with the host and waited for the audience to quit screaming.

The host went through the formalities. Lots of welcoming, joking about how handsome he was, how popular with the ladies. He tensed for a moment, waiting to see if she'd ask him about Constance, but she didn't. Relief flooded him and he relaxed a bit. Maybe she'd actually stick to the list and keep away from the forbidden topics after all.

He was good-naturedly teased about his cameo in an upcoming Adam Sandler movie and then she got down to why he'd wanted to be there in the first place. Excitement zipped through him at finally being able to reveal the project he'd been working on.

"So, Luca, in addition to working alongside your father, you've got a special project of your own in the works, is that right?" the host, a tiny little blond woman, asked him.

"Yes. This has been in the planning stage for a while now and it's a project that is really close to my heart. We've finally gotten the last permissions we need and will be breaking ground in Mykonos on the first Constant Heart Children's Aid Village next week. We are hoping to be able to build many more over the next few years."

"Oh, that's wonderful! Now, these villages are groups of foster homes, essentially, correct?"

"Yes. With the financial crisis hitting so hard, more and more children need good, stable homes in which to live. The foster families who are part of the Family Emergency Aid organization tend to live near one another for support and help. We call these groupings of such homes villages. Unfortunately, it's not always possible to find homes near each other as more and more homes are needed. The Constant Heart Foundation would like to change that by providing these homes for the foster groups."

"What a wonderful goal! But, I have to mention it, as these villages are located in Greece, does this mean you'll be moving there full time to oversee the building?"

A general groan of dismay came from the audience and he laughed like they expected him to. Though the fact that she had glossed right over the plight of these children to focus on where he'd be spending his time infuriated him. "For the most part. I'll still spend some time here in the States and in London, but the bulk of my time will be in Greece for now."

"The Constant Heart Foundation. Quite a poignant name," the host said. "You were engaged not long ago to a social worker..." She checked her notes. "Constance McMurty. That relationship sadly didn't work out, but going by the nature of this project, and the name you've given it, can we assume that there might be some lingering feelings there? Or at least a bit of inspiration?"

Luca's stomach bottomed out. She went where she wasn't supposed to. He'd known this was a distinct possibility, unavoidable probably, considering the fact that Constance *was* his inspiration and he'd named the project after her. Well, he couldn't get out of answering the question without being horribly rude, and Constance was hopefully watching. So be it. He'd seize the opportunity and tell her everything he'd wanted to tell her.

The host sat forward, salivating for every juicy detail. Luca ignored her and just said what was in his heart.

"More than a bit of inspiration. There would be no foundation without her. She is the best example I know of someone who is selfless and good and kind. She introduced me to the work this organization does, something I'm ashamed to say I knew nothing about, though I should have. My life was focused on partying and fame."

"Ah, but there's always a little room for a good party, am I right?" she asked, winking at the audience.

Luca gave her a tight smile. "Within reason. I went a great deal overboard in that regard. Constance changed all that, changed me, made me want to be a better man."

The host sat there momentarily silenced, whether by his sincerity, something she probably rarely saw, or by the seriousness of his words, he wasn't sure.

"Sounds like you still care for her."

Luca took a deep breath. "I'm head over heels in love with her. Have been since the day I met her, and always will be."

The host clutched her chest. "Oh my. That's quite a declaration."

Luca laughed a little and shook his head. "It's something I should have said when I had the chance, but I was stupid, too focused on the wrong things."

He turned toward the camera and looked straight into the lens, praying Constance was somewhere watching.

"Constance, I'm sorry for everything. I didn't arrange for a photographer to be there that night, I swear it. I would never have done something like that. But even still, it was my fault. I wanted to be in the limelight and I made sure I was. I was arrogant to assume I could control it. And I'm sorrier than

I'll ever be able to express for whatever pain your association with me has caused you. I hope you can find it within you to forgive me someday. Whether or not that happens, I want you to know that because of you I've changed. For the better, I hope."

He paused and took a deep breath. "You told me once I had the power to do great things. I hope I can prove you right. I love you, Stanzia. I'll always love you."

He paused for a second, his words sinking in. The host clasped her hand to her chest again.

"That's just…wow," she said, waving at her eyes like she was about to cry although there wasn't a tear in sight.

He glanced at her, but he didn't really see her. He was seeing a woman with dark red hair, flashing blue eyes, and a smile that set his world on fire.

"I love her. Want her. Need her." He shook his head and stood. "And I'm damn well going to go and get her."

He removed his mic and walked off the stage. He hoped Constance had been watching because they belonged together. And he wasn't going to take no for an answer this time.

• • •

Constance sat back, her heart pounding. "Luca," she whispered.

He loved her. He loved her! She couldn't believe it, couldn't believe what he'd just said. What he'd done. He was building villages. All those homes! And he was coming for her.

"Constance! Constance!" Mrs. Ballas ran in, probably from her own house judging by how hard she was breathing. She pressed her hands to her cheeks. "Did you see?"

Constance nodded, still stunned speechless.

"Oh, think of all the children and families we can help now."

"Yes," she said faintly. "It's wonderful."

She couldn't sit there anymore. She had to get up, had to go…somewhere. He was in New York. She couldn't go to him but she could wait for him. He was coming for her. He'd left the studio. Wait…

Up in the corner of the television screen was a little notation saying *Previously Recorded*. The show hadn't been live, which meant he could already be back in Greece, on Mykonos.

"Mrs. Ballas, I…"

The old woman patted her cheek. "I know, dear. I'll hold down the fort here. You go get him."

Constance laughed and swept her into a hug. "Thank you."

She sprinted out the door. She grabbed her moped and was off before she could really process in her mind what her plan was. Sit on his front porch until he came home? If Joseph even let her in the gates. If Joseph was even there. She almost had a slight panic attack before she remembered that Luca had given her the gate and house codes as long as he hadn't changed them. She'd walked out on him months ago. If he'd been smart, he would have changed them. She blew out a breath and gave her scooter more gas. Only one way to find out.

She pulled to a stop in front of his estate. There were no paparazzi around. No female fans hanging out in their cars hoping for a glimpse. She entered the gate code, her heart pounding.

The gate swung open. She drove up to the house and jumped off her moped to run up the front steps, not hesitating this time. Her key still fit the lock; the code still shut off the alarm. Had he left everything as it was, hoping all this time that she'd come back?

She wandered from room to room. Everything was exactly as she'd left it, from the clothing she'd left still hanging in the closet, to her toothbrush in the bathroom, to the basket of the girls' toys in the front room and their bedrooms still set up waiting for them to come home. He'd left it all. Her heart soared. Yes, maybe it was a bit arrogant of him to assume she'd return. Or maybe he just hadn't given up hope.

Would he be hoping that she was there now? Would he come home looking for her?

Or…would he go someplace else? Their place. His secret place. The place that had been the beginning of the end. What better place for a new beginning?

She went back out and got on her scooter. Hopefully she could remember the way. She'd only been the one time and she'd been a bit distracted by the rock-hard Greek god she'd had her thighs wrapped around.

Only one wrong turn later and she found the long dirt path that lead to the bungalow. She realized too late that she didn't have a key. Disappointed, she walked around to the back. The swing bed swayed gently in the breeze and Constance's body tingled with the memories of the night they'd spent there.

The sound of the waves washing ashore called to her. She'd always loved that sound. Especially at dusk, when the sky above the sea turned its brilliant orange and faded slowly into the gentle dark hues of night.

She wandered down the rocky path to the shore, kicking off her sandals once she reached the sand. The salt-tinged air filled her lungs and she took a deep breath, trying to calm her racing mind. What would she say when she saw him again? Could they really make this work? She wasn't sure she cared anymore what their differences were, what obstacles stood in their way. She just wanted to see him again.

She hadn't heard his footsteps in the sand, but the clean,

fresh scent of him announced his presence behind her just before his arms slipped around her waist. He filled her senses, totally and completely, and she leaned back against his chest with a sigh. All the tension she'd carried around for the last few months melted from her. She sighed, at peace at last.

He held her for a few moments as they watched the sun dip lower into the horizon, then he turned her around in his arms. His hands reached up to cup her face, his thumbs brushing across her cheeks.

"You're here," he said.

"Yes." She smiled up at him. "I saw you on the show."

"I hoped you would." He smiled down at her and brushed her hair from her face.

"How did you get here so quickly?"

"The show was taped a few days ago. I arrived this morning and came straight here. It's been a very long day, wondering if you'd let me in again, if you'd let me see you. And here you are." He kissed her forehead, held her close.

"I think I would have come anyway. Living without you these last few months…" She shook her head, tears tightening her throat. "I don't think I could have done it much longer, but I did want to tell you—and I don't know how to say this without sounding like a mother hen—but I wanted to tell you that I'm so proud of you."

"You are?" he said, his tender expression warming her through and through.

"So much. Using your powers for good instead of evil. Not many supermen can pull off a switch like that."

He laughed and hugged her again. "God, I love you so much."

His arms enveloped her, crushed her to him like he'd never let go. She wrapped her arms around his waist, her heart so full of love for him she could scarcely breathe.

"I love you," she said, pulling away enough to reach his

face. "I should have told you before." She stood on tiptoe and kissed his cheeks, his brow, his lips, all the while whispering, "I love you, I love you," over and over again.

He crushed her to him with a sound that was almost a sob, his lips capturing hers. He kissed her until she was breathless and dizzy before he released her with a ragged sigh.

"Don't ever leave me again," he said, leaning his forehead against hers.

"Never," she agreed.

He pulled back so he could look into her eyes. "You know what that means? I've done what I can to stay out of the spotlight, but there will always be photographers. There will always be private details splashed in the papers. My life will always be a little bit…crazy."

"I know," she said, smiling up at him. "I'm not saying I'll enjoy all that, but it's a small price to pay to be with the man I love."

The smile he bestowed upon her took her breath away.

"Are you sure?"

She nodded. "Never been more sure of anything in my life."

"Then maybe I should give this back to you." He pulled her sapphire ring out of his pocket. "My strong, amazing, beautiful Stanzia… Marry me. For real this time."

She laughed, so full of happiness she was sure it radiated from every pore. "Yes," she said, her heart nearly jumping from her chest when he slipped the ring back on her finger.

He lifted her hand to his lips and kissed the ring. "And you'll move back into the house tonight. I'm not letting you out of my sight."

She laughed and then gasped, her stomach dropping. "Wait. I can't."

Luca's face fell, his eyes widening.

"I want to," she insisted, "I do. But…the girls…I can't

leave them…"

"Oh," he said, letting out a sigh of relief and crushing her to him again. "God, you scared me." He gave her a lingering kiss. "Don't worry about the girls. I still have everything all set up for them. I don't see any reason why the Family Aid organization wouldn't approve me as a House Father, especially if you remain the House Mother. The girls were living with me anyway."

"Luca, are you sure?"

"I've never been more sure of anything in my life. I want all my girls back home where they belong."

"Oh, Luca," she said, giving him a swift kiss. "Thank you so much."

"Let's sit for a second." He pulled her down to the sand with him, tucking her into his chest with his arms wrapped about her and his legs on either side, keeping her cocooned from the cool breeze blowing in off the sea. "There's something else I wanted to discuss with you."

He still seemed happy, but there was something beneath the surface. He almost seemed nervous, anxious about something. "What is it?" she asked with a slight frown.

"I wanted to see how you'd feel about making some of the arrangements permanent. I mean more so than they already are."

"What do you mean?" She thought she knew, but she was afraid to hope that much.

"If it would be all right with you, and with her, I'd like for us to adopt Elena."

Constance gasped and flipped around in his arms, wrapping her legs around his waist so she could hug him with her whole body. "Oh Luca, of course it's okay with me. I never dreamed…" She pulled away to look at him though his smiling face was blurry through her tears. "Really?"

"Really," he said with a little laugh. "I've sown enough

wild oats."

She snorted and he gave her a mock glare. "I think it's time I settled down and had a family, and I always was one for instant gratification."

She laughed. "Well, just this once, my love, I wholeheartedly approve."

"Good," he said, jumping up, bring her along with him. "Let's go get our girls."

Constance tugged on his hand, drawing him back to her. She reached up to cup his face, drawing him down for a kiss. "Mrs. Ballas is in charge for the night. You and I have some catching up to do."

His smile turned sensual, desire flashing through his eyes. "I love the way you think, *koritsi mou*."

# Author's Note

The Emergency Family Aid organization that Constance works for in this story is loosely based on a real organization, SOS Children's Villages International. The SOS organization provides homes and care for children whose families are no longer able to do so. While elements similar to the real organization were used for this book, literary license was taken to fit the needs of the story. For more information on the real SOS Children's Villages, please visit their website at http://www.sos-childrensvillages.org.

# Acknowledgments

My deepest thanks to the entire Entangled team, especially my incredible editor, Alethea Spiridon. Luca wouldn't be here without you, and without Luca my world would be tragic. Thank you so much for everything. I have loved working with you and appreciate everything you've done to get this book out in the world.

To my sweet husband, who makes me breathe fresh air, cooks real food, tells me I look great even when I'm on deadline and look like an extra on *The Walking Dead*, and only rarely fusses when I stumble into bed just before he gets up—I really couldn't do this without you. At least not well. Just imagine how pale I'd be if it weren't for you dragging me out into the sun every now and then.

To my amazing kids, for never complaining no matter how many pizza days or video games you're forced to endure, for scattering when I need a few extra work minutes and still putting up with the Mama Love even though you're almost as tall as I am—you are my everything. And I promise to put on my "outside clothes" before I pick you up at school. Most of the time.

To Sarah Ballance, my writing creepy twin who somehow manages to keep me sane with your crazy (our crazy?)—my family thanks you. Without you, they'd have to deal with me unfiltered and I'm not sure they are up to that. Also, keep your spiders to yourself. I see a spider, I'm breaking out the mice. Fair warning. As for the jalepeno chips, address them to my son. The kid was drinking salsa when he was two. He thanks you in advance. I wonder if anyone has noticed we talk to each other in these things yet…this could get interesting.

And most importantly, to my fabulous readers. You are the reason I can do what I do. I can't even express what that means to me. You guys are beyond wonderful!

# About the Author

Kira Archer resides in Pennsylvania with her husband, two kiddos, and far too many animals in the house. She tends to laugh at inappropriate moments, break all the rules she gives her kids (but only when they aren't looking), and would rather be reading a book than doing almost an-ything else. She has odd, eclectic tastes in just about everything and often let's her imagination run away with her. She loves a vast variety of genres and writes in quite a few. If you love his-torical romances, check out her alter ego, Michelle McLean.